Twilight Terrors

A Collection Of Ghost Stories

Edited By
Jenni Blood-curdling Bannister

First published in Great Britain in 2011 by:

 Young**Writers**

Young Writers
Remus House
Coltsfoot Drive
Peterborough
PE2 9BF
Telephone: 01733 890066
Website: www.youngwriters.co.uk

Foreword

Young Writers was established in 1991 to promote poetry and nurture the creative writing talent in school children across the UK and overseas. Today we continue to provide a platform for children and young adults to showcase their work. Our ghost story competition has proved so popular over the last few years that it has become an open competition. Now we receive hundreds of stories all year round and publish 4 or 5 ghost story books a year!

Twilight Terrors is a collection of ghost stories that will certainly give you the creeps! From friendly ghosts and Halloween adventures to the gruesome and macabre, the young writers in this anthology showcase their story-telling talents. The best ghost story wins a family ticket to either London, York or Edinburgh Dungeons, with 2 runners-up each winning some Staedtler stationery and a selection of books. Congratulations to our winners, and thank you to all our authors for being part of this fantastic anthology.

Contents

Winner
Rachel Halsall (15) 1

Runners Up
Zohra Khan (9) 2
Joseph Foster (16) 3

Independent Entries
Alicia Williamson (8) 4
Charley Gledhill (10).................................. 5
Courtney Moore (10) 6
Luke McKee (11) 7
Jake Bairstow (10)..................................... 8
Theo Allotey (10) 9
Yasmin Colstock (10).................................. 10
Lydia Kate Coyle (11) 11
Samuel Dunkley (11) 12
Chloe Crosswaite (10) 13
Jack Terry (10)... 14
Toluwani Asalu 15
Josh Oldroyd (10)..................................... 16
Rebecca Booth (10)................................... 17
Precious Olaniyi (10) 18
Robyn Hill (14).. 19
Marcus McCabe (12) 20
Demi Adetoro (13) 21
Ayesha Noor (15) 22
Taylor Dadswell (10).................................. 23
Gopija Nanthangopan (12) 24
Eleanor Craker (18) 25
Sophia Ellie Simpson (11) 26
Theo Collin (12) 27
Sian Lloyd (11).. 28
Regan Mulcahy (13) 29
Jessica Owen (13) 30
Jessica Deacon (13)................................... 31
Isabelle Kenyon (14)................................. 32
Jasmine Hadley (11).................................. 33
Lisa Head (13) 34
Elliot Elstob (15) 35
Katrina Larsen-Kittle (11).......................... 36

Lee Sutton (13).. 37
Hibiki-Hitomi Sakuta (8).......................... 38
Josie Bristow-Booker (9) 39
Morgan Rusted (12)................................... 40
Usman Irfan (14)...................................... 41
Daniel Penney-Gallagher (11) 42
Elizabeth Rose Facer (13)......................... 43
Subah Sabur (12) 44
Nadia Madoui (13) 45
Maisie Dixon (11)..................................... 46
Arnold Lincoln (12) 47
Blythe Rachael Britz (12).......................... 48
Rachel Tookey (17)................................... 49
Aimeé Louisa Parris (12) 50
Alice Shaw (12) 51
Ruhama Gill (12) 52
Vanessa Ezeugwa (12)............................... 53
Katrina Jan (16)....................................... 54
Rowan Smith (11) 55
Freya Christina Smith (11) 56
Jodie Marsden (12)................................... 57
Micaela Arroyo Zugarramurdi (14).......... 58
Thandiwe Tafireyi (17) 59
Serena Arthur (12) 60
Mandeep Bal (16) 61
Thomas Taylor (12)................................... 62
Rabiat Umar (13) 63
Stephanie Louise Sargent (9)................... 64
Joe Hardwick (12)..................................... 65
Destiny Butler-Cook (12) 66
Gabbie Hubbard (12)................................. 67
Florence Nicholson-Lailey (10).............. 68
Charlotte Ash (10).................................... 69
Cora Diamond (11) 70
Sharnise Craig (11)................................... 72
Charlotte Groves (16)............................... 73
Amy Kirkland (12)..................................... 74
Hannah Chandler (16)............................... 75
Amy Chandler (11).................................... 76
Habibah Dukandar (10) 77
Sannah Shah (11)...................................... 78

Shannon Bevan (9)...................................79
Hirra Mahmood (15) 80
Daphne Siapno (13) 81
Megan Elliot (12) 82
Emma Jones (14) 83
Tom Barnes (7)..................................... 84
Julia Barnes (7) 85
Jahmal Taylor (10)............................... 86
Annie Charalambous (10)..................... 87
Thaiba Hussain (15) 88
Tom Rowell (16)................................... 89
Eleanor Oliver (14) 90
Emmeline Bryce (12) 91
Will Maule (12)..................................... 92
Ross Millen (12)................................... 93
Hannah Glover (11) 94
Emily Jane Knight (14) 95
Molly Cascarina (11)............................ 96
Holly Elliott (14) 97
Charlie Willis (16) 98
Ellie Ackroyd (12)................................ 99
Bryan Neermul (10) 100
Melisa Kaplanbasoglu (11) 101
Adem Hilmi (10)................................. 102
Andrea Caroline Pratt (14).................. 103
Maya Sofia Crasmaru (6) 104
Abbi Davies (12)................................ 105
Josh Brookes (12) 106
Jessica Groom (10) 107
Karvya Kaneswaran (8)....................... 108
Ally Laver (18) 109
Mitch Gleed (12).................................110

Benfield School, Newcastle Upon Tyne

Leah McMillan (13)...............................111
Joe Lowrey (12)...................................112
Jake Smith...113
Brooke Gibson (13) 114
Rhiannon Bell (13)...............................116

Carr Hill High School, Preston

Susan Newton (14)...............................117
Bethany Ackers (13) 118

Corona Secondary School, Nigeria

Chisom Adaeze Egwuatu (11) 119
Tomilola Kosoko (12)........................... 120
Dumebi Vanessa Okoh (12) 122
Etinosa Victor Osaikhuwhomwan (12).. 123

Cyril Jackson Primary School, Limehouse

Anjum Mamon (10)............................... 124
Louie Keir (10)..................................... 125
Yasin Samad (10) 126
Sultan Ahmed (10)............................... 127
Ashfaq Choudhury (10) 128

Diss High School, Diss

Ed Budds (13)..................................... 129
Kia Duly (14)....................................... 130
Thomas Dowden (14) 131
Mary Lambert (14)............................... 132
David Phillips (13)................................ 133
Theo Perrin (13) 134
Aaron O'Brien (14).............................. 135
Jessica Cooper (14) 136
Evan Hughes (13)................................ 137

The Creative Writing

Well done Rachel!

Congratulations Rachel, your creepy short story wins you a fantastic family ticket to The Dungeons! These fantastic places are filled with grisly exhibitions and examples of atrocities from British and European history. The museums appeal to our morbid curiosity, but be warned - they are not recommended to those with a nervous disposition or squeamish nature!

Chilling tales from our history are re-enacted, providing eerie, atmospheric fun for those brave enough to enter. Delve into the blood-curdling parts of history often overlooked as they are so gruesome - learn about the grisly methods of Jack the Ripper in London's Dungeon to the infamous legend of Dick Turpin at York. Whichever location you choose to visit, The Dungeons offers visitors a thrill like no other attraction. For more info visit www.thedungeons.com.

Bad Dreams

I had a nightmare last night. I dreamt that I was lying in bed, almost on the brink of sleep. My eyes drooped and my mind was dull with exhaustion. But just as I started to doze I felt something climb up on the bed and settle itself upon my chest, pinning me down with its dead weight. I was unable to move an inch. I could do nothing but lie there in paralysed horror as papery hands scuttled over my face and prised my jaws apart. It took my tongue between its fingers and tore it out in a shower of blood. I was almost blinded with agony. Satisfied with my pain, the thing on my chest leaned forward and whispered something into my ear.

I don't know what it said, but whatever it was filled me with such an unearthly terror that I screamed like an infant. The last thing I remember before jerking awake was the creature stuffing my mouth with bundles of twigs a-crawl with woodlice.

I wish I could say it was only a dream but that isn't true. Upon brushing my teeth this morning I found tree bark stuck to my lips and a row of thick, black stitches lining the back of my tongue.

I don't want to think about it anymore. Just recalling the incident makes me feel sick with fear. But I can't help it. I'm convinced that when I fall asleep tonight that thing will be there, waiting for me.

Rachel Halsall (15)

The Curse Begins

Sirens made a terrible racket all around. Helicopters shone their blinding light, searching for the hasty criminal.

It was the dead of night when the incident happened, when the curse first began.

Leaping over the rooftops one by one, dodging each net that was thrown down, making his way through the icy air and force of mist, running, sprinting for his life.

Alas, he made his way through. He landed directly beneath the moon, the stars shining so bright, his fangs shone like a thousand clear diamonds. *Bang, bang*, his boots hit the floor as he arrived at his kingdom. His dark brown, muddy boot trail made the shiny tiles across the ground an ugly sight.

The Master had returned to his castle laughing an evil laugh. It got louder by the minute, more evil by the second and more deadly with each tick of the second-hand on the ancient grandfather clock. Something though, something was different. Something made the air thin all around. The laugh had frozen like a lake in the middle of winter and then the silence commenced.

The Master had frozen like the lake and no one moved for one hundred years.

After that time people were warned that the curse still runs through the frozen veins of The Master ...

Zohra Khan (9)

(Prize may differ from illustration shown.)

Well done Zohra!

Your scary story wins you a selection of books and some **STAEDTLER** stationery.

Vainlarn's Revenge

'It's said if you lay silent, place your ear to the wind, the sounds of a thousand lost lie whispering upon the breeze.' - Captain Vainlarn.

Waves thundered upon the hull, gently rocking our ship back and forth in perfect 4/4 timing. I always loved storms. The engrossing beauty of nature flittering upon the fine line of unparalleled perfection and a watery grave. I sat up from my cottons and stared out to sea from the porthole which lay next to me. An endless barrage of black, almost tar-like water distorted my view.

I stood up from my bed, swayed toward the seemingly ancient drinks cabinet, and nabbed myself a bottle of Vainlarn's special.

'Mutiny, it's a terrible thing,' I chuckled to myself. 'Though I'm not sure hanging his body upon the mast was entirely necessary.' I trundled toward my bed once more and sat upon its fine linen, though something was now different. It was ... silent.

A stream of a crimson liquid began to run under the door. 'Twas blood.

My hand began to shake, causing me to drop my now unwanted beverage. I walked toward the splintered cabin door. The floorboards creaked as if to warn me of my fate. I turned the cold brass handle, feeling almost like fire to the skin.

The door flung open ...

A chilling blue face met mine ... a figure of unimaginable evil ... it was Vainlarn.

Joseph Foster (16)

(Prize may differ from illustration shown.)

Well done Joseph!

Your scary story wins you a selection of books and some **STAEDTLER** stationery.

Casper

Casper lives in a haunted castle with his evil brother Sean. In other stories Casper is a good little ghost but in this story he's not. Anyway, if anyone tries to make a fortune by taking a photo of Casper and Sean they grab you and put you in a cell.

One cloudy day a bright young girl went with her father to scare away the ghost.

That evening they met the ghosts. For the first time they made friends. Casper found out the strange girl's name - Wendy. Sean found out her father's name - Terry. They did everything together. Swam together, played together, talked together.

For one night only there was a ball. Casper, Sean, Wendy and Terry danced all night together. After that they ate a big chocolate cake together. Casper and Sean became good little ghosts in the end.

Alicia Williamson (8)

Welcome To Horror

Dong ... *dong.* Midnight had struck. I knew something or someone was going to get me. All of a sudden I heard a noise. 'Come here.'

I ran very, very quickly to a house, not an ordinary house, a very haunted house! But then I came to a gate where spikes were as sharp as razor blades. Suddenly another noise came, this was the end!

I looked ... I couldn't believe my eyes; the gates were talking to me. I ran through the gates knowing nothing. I was terrified. A shiver ran up my spine.

Bang! I jumped when suddenly I fell down a deep, deep hole.

'Is this the end?' I said to myself. Was it?

Charley Gledhill (10)

Welcome To Hell!

One dark, stormy night I was walking home from school. All of a sudden a gate whispered to me, 'Come, destiny awaits you.' It can't, can it?

The leaves of the trees were crunching. I could hear them talking to me, very, very slowly. 'Run away … run away, your death is near!'

It was almost Halloween; I knew not to go near. My heart was telling me to go back home but the wind kept blowing me towards the door. I was nervous, my friend was coming with me, she was excited. But then I knocked on the door. I turned to face my friend … she was gone! She was screaming like a wolf howling.

As I went to go hear and find her, I could near her voice. Then the gate was opening and closing. I was scared. As I went through the woods I could hear bats all around so I could not hear my friend anymore. What will happen next?

Courtney Moore (10)

Hell House

I got home, something was wrong, but what?
I walked into the house. My mum was nowhere to be seen. Where was she? Was she in the kitchen? Then suddenly I heard something outside. I slowly went out but then I saw a strange thing in the garden. It was the end. The Devil had been born! I heard screams of people everywhere and people were disappearing through the floor.

I ran back into my house. There was my mum lying on the floor, blood pouring out of her mouth. My dad was gone too, was it the end for me? Then suddenly something came through the floor and grabbed me. I was slowly disappearing, my end had come.

Nobody knew what happened on that day but the human race was gone and a new race began.

Luke McKee (11)

Midsomer Murders

Dong … dong! Midnight had come. I was woken by a nightmare saying, 'You shall die!'

In the far distance there was something with red eyes, a black back and a long body. I decided to explore.

I heard something howl. 'Hooooo!' The floorboards were creaking. I opened the door. I was terrified. The thing I saw was our dog. It pounced on me. I squashed its pulse and I ran and shouted, 'Mum! Mum!'

'I'm in the kitchen.'

I slammed the door. My mum was stuck in the oven! I yelled, 'Help! Help!' I put my hand on the handle; I felt a soft but slimy hand. I was terrified. I didn't know what to do. Just then something or someone grabbed me. They held me. Was this the end? No! The monster or alien chucked me into the oven. Luckily the oven didn't work. Soon it would be daylight. Just then a creepy and slimy maggot crawled into my ear, it was taking over me. Will I survive?

Jake Bairstow (10)

To Be Able To Write A Ghost Story

One day I was stumbling through the woods. The clock ticked *dong, dong.* Night had come. The gate whispered to me, *'If you want find out more you will have to read on, ha, ha, ha.'*

I saw something white and it was a red, wrinkly hand. I ran and then I tripped! I saw someone coming out of the door of a haunted house. She had a long pointy nose with a huge spot. It was green like snot. I was terrified! I shivered like the wind.

The next day my friend and I were playing at the haunted house. My friend suddenly flew back like a devil had gone into him. He said, 'I have to rest outside.' I went back home the same way as I came.

The next day I called for my friend, his mum came to the door, she said, 'I thought he was with you.'

I went back to the haunted house. I looked through the window; there was blood on the wall! My friend dragged me into the kitchen and he said, 'I can't control myself.' I ran away then I heard a noise saying, 'Help!' I ran back in and he was dead.

The door said, 'You're next!' The door opened. I walked closer, it was a room, it had nails and they were as sharp as a knife and my feet were glued to the floor. Was this the end of me?

Theo Allotey (10)

The Twelfth Strike

Dong ... *dong* ... the clock had struck, midnight had come. I looked around in despair. The clown that hung on my wardrobe once a toy, a memory of fun, glared at me with its tired eyes.

Suddenly the room shook. The puppet fell. It appeared at my feet. It laughed at my petrified face. Would this be the end? I scrambled to find my quilt then dived underneath and prayed this would not be my last breath. My heart was racing. I told myself, 'Breathe, just breathe.' I looked ... 'Argh!' Silence once again. I was gone!

I'm now forced to live an invisible, unreal existence. My only communication is through the howl of the wind and the creak of the doors. I write this to warn you, my friend, beware of the painted face!

Yasmin Colstock (10)

The Haunted House

I was walking home from school on a dark and stormy night. It felt like I was being watched. My heart was beating faster and faster. I could hear footsteps behind me. I started to run. The footsteps got quicker and turned into a run. I had to hide. There was an old abandoned house. Everyone said that it was haunted, but it was my only option.

As I ran through the door it shut and creaked. This was the end! I had to hide. I ran and hid under the stairs. It was pitch-black. I was just about to breathe a sigh of relief when I saw, in the back of the cupboard, two red piercing eyes. I screamed! But no one ever heard me!

Lydia Kate Coyle (11)

Hell Or Death?

I was walking home. No one was out. Unusual, or was it? I kept on going, got out my keys then stopped. I looked at my house … Oh my God! 16 Thilmere Drive was Hell!

I walked forward and saw my mum, continually knocking on the window, my dad, stuck on the satellite, and my sister like a hollow empty shell.

I went inside. Everything changed. It was a perfect house … *bang!*

Then the house changed. There was a button guarded by many weapons sticking out and coming back in very fast. Luckily I was good at dodgeball and gymnastics. I jumped, flipped, dodged and ducked.

'Ouch! One of the blades cut me!' I finally got to the end and pressed the red button. Everything changed, everything was perfect.

'Sam!' shouted Mrs Thompson. 'Stop daydreaming!'

'Sorry Miss but I've got a really good idea for that ghost story competition. I'll explain …'

Samuel Dunkley (11)

My Night In Hell

A re you ready for the truth of what really happens in Hell?
Last week I was playing football with my friend, Nathan. I kicked the ball into a garden which had thorns and leaves all over. As I walked nearer to it I heard whispering saying, 'Don't come near or you will disappear.'

I opened the gate and ran for the ball then suddenly I couldn't move my feet. The weeds and thorns were pushing the ball closer and closer to the door. They pushed it and I lost control of my feet. It was like I was getting dragged towards the door. As I was getting pulled nearer the door it shut on the ball and it popped. I thought, *is that going to happen to me?*

I tried stopping myself from going near the door. Luckily, when I got one more step nearer to the door, I had gained back control of my feet. As I ran into the house the door slammed behind me. I ran into the living room and sat on the sofa. Suddenly I was sinking into the sofa!

When I got myself out of that trouble the walls started leaking blood and it dripped into letter shapes. It said, 'I warned you!'

I ran into the kitchen. When I got into the kitchen the paint deformed, it said, 'You can run but you can't hide.'

I ran out of the back door. The weeds and thorns picked me up and threw me into a grave with five skeletons. I felt them ripping my skin apart. I knew this was the end.

Chloe Crosswaite (10)

Untitled

Sometimes you may get scared of spiders but that's nothing compared to what happened to me. I'll explain as much as I can.

One day I was walking home from school and horror had struck me. I saw a gate with a mouth! It was saying, 'Don't come in! Don't come in! You'll never survive!' When I was a kid I was a little naughty so I entered.

Well, when I entered I couldn't believe what I saw. I saw a little boy being devoured by rats and bats. It was like a lion blasting furious claws at him, it was that bad. In three seconds the boy was bone dry. I screamed! I was so scared. The door shut with a loud *bang!*

'Bye-bye,' said the dead kid.

'Argh!' I shouted in horror. Would I die?

I am writing to you from the grave, now that's scary!

Jack Terry (10)

A Road Trip To Hell

As I walked down that dark alley I came towards abandoned houses. Suddenly the gates awoke and pushed me into the death trap.

My legs were dragging me into the house. The door closed quietly, trapping me in its arms. The windows stared at me in spite. I could hear someone, or something, trying to grab me. I would never have freedom ever again. Then there was sudden silence.

Someone jumped on me, trying to steal my soul. I was thinking deadly thoughts. I saw bloodstains on the walls from the people who had died there but yet they were still alive. Was it my end? Would I live to see another day?

Then I was left to die on the floor with only my oranges left to keep me alive. Was it over? Was it my fault? My curiosity took over me.

Toluwani Asalu

The House Over The Road

In 1980 there was a big purple house. The man who lived there cried at the council. 'Please, please, help!' he begged. 'Please destroy this house.'

The council said, 'No!' Then he screamed while his skin ripped and his organs exploded. The council didn't listen.

Thirty years later when everyone had forgotten, a man bought the house and lived there. Seven days later he heard squeaks downstairs. He murmured, 'Damn mice!'

The morning after he bought a cat to catch the mice.

Next morning the cat was on the floor, bone dry. He stared in horror. He called his friend to have a look at it. Squeaks and rattles began. He and his friend saw the wall turn blood-red. The man and his friend ran outside. He didn't make it. His friend was outside waiting.

The fact about this story is no one knows if he is alive but all we know is that house was empty … till now.

Josh Oldroyd (10)

The Haunted House

One dark Halloween night I was exploring the woods. The leaves were rustling, the wind was whistling and glowing eyes were gleaming in the dark. Owls were hooting here and there.

All of a sudden I heard moaning from the graves. *The ghosts have risen from the grave,* I thought. Suddenly I heard rustling from behind. My heart was pounding. I ran for my life! I looked back to find that someone was stalking me; they had a knife! I ran faster than ever.

Finally I lost sight of him. I looked around then there in front of me was a haunted house guarded by a huge black gate. The gate sounded like it was saying, 'Don't go any closer or the ghosts will get you.'

I took a great big breath and entered the garden, even if the gate warned me I was still curious. So I rang the doorbell … *dong … dong.* Then the door creaked open. I took a deep breath and stepped into the haunted house.

'Hello? Is anybody there?' I asked in a quivery voice.

As I tiptoed further into the house the door slammed behind me, the curtains shut and the lights turned off. I started to breathe heavily. I felt my way through the house. All of a sudden I felt a cold shiver down my spine as if someone was breathing on me …

Rebecca Booth (10)

The Magical Crystal

As I went upstairs it was raining heavily and thunder and lightning struck. I ran upstairs and hid under my blanket. I was terrified. Before I knew it I had fallen asleep.

I was woken when the storm became louder and suddenly something landed on my blanket. I saw something on my blanket, I saw a bright shining crystal and it shone like the sun so I picked it up and before I knew it I had disappeared.

I was in a universe. It was dark. There were weird noises everywhere. I was terrified when a man jumped out with an axe and his face was covered with blood. I almost jumped out of my skin.

He said, 'Prepare to meet your doom!' I screamed with fear and I ran as fast as I could.

As I ran I bumped into a tree. 'Hello.'

I shivered with fear as the tree picked me up and said again, 'Prepare to meet your doom!' It swallowed me!

But it wasn't the end of me, the tree threw me away. I stood up and I saw myself in the middle of the haunted house gate, it was Hell! It looked spooky and huge. I was terrified!

The gate whispered and said, 'Come in, come in.' It opened. I was too scared to go inside. The gate whispered again, 'It will lead you back home.' So I went in.

I heard a big bang so turned around. The gate was shut. I ran to it and I tried to open it. The gate disappeared before my very eyes. The skeletons came out of their graves. They came close and closer and they grabbed my crystal and as I watched it break they grabbed me and dragged me into the grave.

I heard a loud bang as 12 o'clock struck, but was it the end?

Precious Olaniyi (10)

My Heart Skips A Beat

Walking through the empty, silent, dark alleyway on my own with a torch in my left hand and pepper spray in the other, clattering sounds coming from every direction due to cats scrounging for food. *Bang!* My heart skips a beat.

I drop everything from my hands onto the floor and I collapse slowly onto my knees. I look up and see some kind of figure running away.

'Help!' I scream. No one hears me, I feel alone and ever so scared. Still on my knees I put my hands on my stomach and I look down at my bloody hands. Shaking as I start to lie down on this damp muddy road and tears start to come down my fragile face, I curl up and listen to the noises of the city.

I hear a voice in the distance. I shout help again. Footsteps start getting closer. A man-like figure appears through the mist. He puts his hand into his leathery black jacket. I close my eyes and wait …

Robyn Hill (14)

Hauntingly Inevitable

Dudley crept down the balding stairs and swept past the couple as they ate breakfast, on through to the lounge. Nobody looked up. Feeling bored, Dudley turned the telly on, volume low. 'Ahhh,' he sighed, slumping into a crumbling armchair.

Moments later a man waddled in. 'Dear,' he called, 'did you leave the TV on? We really need to save electricity,' he muttered, double chins jogging along to his every word.

His wife joined him and turned the telly back on - some dreadful reality show.

Dudley was forced to retire to the kitchen. Perched on a stool, he stared hard at the last piece of caramel fudge cake, wishing that he could eat it. Suddenly he noticed a flame snaking its way along the tea towel draped across the hob. Dudley knew what it was like to be caught in a fire. He skidded into the sitting room. How to alert them?

He turned the TV off but the man just fiddled with the remote. He knocked the woman's glasses off the elbow of the armchair, but she just frowned at her own elbow. Then Dudley picked up the glasses and waved them desperately in front of the woman's face. Now both husband and wife were clutching each other and whimpering, but they stayed rooted to the sofa. Just then, the fiery blaze slithered round into the room ... It roared as it caught the highly flammable carpet.

'I tried to t-t-tell you,' stammered Dudley to the two new ghosts.

Marcus McCabe (12)

Lost

'Luke, where are you? It's not funny,' said Ella uncertainly. She'd been looking for her brother for an hour and by the minute getting more and more frightened.

It was nearly 11pm and it was pitch-black outside, which made the house look bigger and more threatening than ever. It was a wintry January evening and the wind howled outside bringing with it sounds that Ella preferred to block out.

Bang! Ella's head immediately turned upwards and her heart started to pound so loudly she felt certain that it would come out of her ears. Ella debated what to do in her head, she first thought of just ignoring the noise and sleeping downstairs on the sofa, but then she thought of the trouble that she would get into when her parents got home and were one child short.

Ella cautiously approached the staircase as though she were trying to sneak up on someone, which for all she knew she could be. As she trod on the first step an almighty squeak filled the house, scaring Ella.

She finally arrived at the top of the stairs. Something warm and thick dripped onto the back of her neck. She reached to touch it but when she saw her hand she screamed, 'Argh!' and ran down the stairs and out of the front door without even stopping to get her shoes.

In the house, sitting in the attic, was Luke clutching a pot of red paint and rolling across the floor laughing.

Demi Adetoro (13)

The Beach

I grasped his hands tighter as we forced our way against the vicious waves. Trembling, I handed him over to the vicious monsters that awaited him. Betrayal. Shocked screams that strolled in the night sky slowly faded with the calm tide.

Laughter burst into the atmosphere, grabbing my attention, as young women with splodges of shocking pink blusher flushed across their burned faces, lay giggling, absorbing the heat of the scorching sun. The sound of sinister seagulls in the distance echoes in my head again and again like a stuck CD. My heart pounds with guilt and fear as my imagination of the waves attacking many innocent lives, strike me like a bolt of lightning.

The bitter taste of salt roams around with the minty breeze, leaving me thirsting for a minute drop of sour bitterness to burst in my mouth with flavour. Nothing. My dry mouth begs for some kind of excitement as I try to deceive it with the flavour of my saliva. The ferocious wind blows minute golden biscuit crumbles into my eyes, causing tiny crystal-like tears to drip down my sweaty face as my eyelashes flutter helplessly in defence. How can one small spec of sand cause so much agony and pain?

The betrayal of love leaves me guilty with the feeling of being a murderer. Wiping my priceless tears, I realise it's too late, what drowned with the tide that day can never be reborn again but it will haunt me for the rest of my life like a ghost.

Ayesha Noor (15)

The Thing!

That was it, Emily could feel it. A shiver ran down her spine making her shudder. What would it do to her? Eat her? Rip her to shreds or maybe do nothing to her … just torment her for the rest of her life. Emily struggled to think of such disturbing thoughts; she didn't know what to do, if she could stand it any longer. She was more scared than she ever had been … in her life. What could she do? Maybe run into her parents' room? No, too risky. Emily felt like her world was ending, every second closer. She had to face her fears.

Emily climbed out of bed and within seconds she was gone!

Taylor Dadswell (10)

Sweet Revenge

All he could see was darkness; this was his punishment for burning his master's dinner. Locked out of the house, in the depth of the woods, all alone, with no one to talk to for who knows how long. Or was he alone? If he listened carefully a distant swishing noise could be heard, like the sound of a long cloak's hem dragging across the earthy floor. *Crack!* What was that? It sounded like a twig snapping underfoot, was someone coming towards him?

He had heard rumours about the ghost of Sir Henry who roamed the forest looking for his murderer who had shot an arrow through his heart. The night smothered him, he couldn't breathe for fright. Shivering, he stood there, ghosts didn't exist, only fools believed in ghosts. Was he a fool? He couldn't quite bring himself to answer this mental question.

Snap! Not another twig. Now a distant muttering could be heard.

With a burst of adrenaline he realised what was being said. 'Let me kill you, let me rip you, tear you to bits. Sweet revenge is mine, I see you now, do you see me?'

Moments later a hazy form appeared in front of the boy. The ghost was wearing a bloodstained cloak and an arrow was sticking out of Sir Henry's chest. The cold black eyes glinted with a hint of madness then met him and all he could do was scream as the arrow plunged deep into his own heart.

Gopija Nanthangopan (12)

Lionel

'Are you a ghost?' was the first thing I asked the boy who walked through the hospital room wall. He nodded.

'I'm Lionel,' he said. 'And the short story is that you, Floyd, are dead and there's something out to get you.'

Now I wouldn't normally go off with a stranger who walks into my hospital room, but this guy was a ghost, he knew my name and I'd just woken up from a coma so my brain was slightly muddled.

'I'm dead? I'm a ghost?'

'Dead isn't that bad.'

'Actually,' I began, but Lionel was staring over my shoulder.

'There are other things to worry about, right now.'

I turned around. Nothing there.

'Hide,' Lionel pulled me straight through the side of a cupboard.

'What are they? What do … '

'Quiet!'

The air turned icy. My skin prickled. Lionel inched closer, tense, shaking.

With a chalk-on-blackboard noise, long skeletal fingers pushed through the wood of the cupboard door. They reached around, joints clicking and creaking, hooked nails scratching softly against the wood. Something bumped against the outside of the cupboard and I choked back a whimper.

'What?'

Lionel clapped a hand over my mouth.

The fingers withdrew. Then the tapping began, all over the cupboard walls. *Click, click, click.* The fingers explored our hiding place, catching on something. Then, with a terrible ripping sound, the wood in one corner began to splinter.

'I'm sorry,' Lionel said and vanished, just as the side of the cupboard was torn away.

Eleanor Craker (18)

Revenge Is Death!

One dark, gloomy night a man called Tom received a phone call saying his close friend John had sadly passed away. John had worked with Tom for thirty years. That night was Friday the 13th and Tom didn't yet know that ever since the phone call ear-piercing noises filled the dim, dark room.

All of a sudden a black silhouette of a man appeared. It was John; he had come back for his thirty years of revenge.

'I can see you Tom, I can see you,' whispered John's ghost.

Tom screamed for help.

'You killed me Tom Buttery, you killed me! Thirty years of your moaning, thirty years. Now it's your turn Tom, your turn.'

John killed Tom.

Sophia Ellie Simpson (11)

Welcome To Chiller Land

There I was, entering the abandoned haunted house at Chiller Land. As I walked through the ancient, smashed doors the candles flickered on and off.

All of a sudden the door slammed shut and there was someone singing in the room in front of me! I stood as still as a building, wondering what it was until it stopped and cried. It started to come closer to the gloomy, destroyed door, still muttering under its breath. Suddenly claws as sharp as needles appeared, clutching the wood of the door! It appeared, gave out a terrible scream and ran forwards!

20 minutes before …

I walked into the shiny, colourful entrance of Chiller Land, the new theme park that made your fears alive! Mum muttered darkly whilst Dad was scribbling a bunch of words on a piece of paper. Molly (my little two-year-old sister) was fast asleep in her gigantic buggy as well as her teddy, Ted, because Molly doesn't leave him alone.

We walked down the packed walkway to the haunted house, also the gibberish roller coaster. As we got to the entrance to the haunted house Molly woke with an ear-bursting scream so I begged my mum to let me go in the ghostly house! When she nodded her head I ran into the monstrous house. As I entered the house no one else was inside so I wandered in! All of a sudden the door slammed and someone was singing in the room in front! I stopped still! Heart pounding, what was that?

Theo Collin (12)

The Dead Boy's Closet

One morning five boys went to an abandoned house because they dared their friend to go in the house and stay in the closet for thirty minutes.

'I don't want to go in, you know what people say about that house,' said Tim.

'What's that story?' said John.

'Ten years ago there was a family living in the house. The mother and the father were abusing their son. They hit him and when they had done enough damage to him, they locked him in his closet. He screamed to get out but his parents just ignored him … and now his ghost haunts that closet!' said Jack.

'Fine, I'll do it but only if someone comes with me,' said Tim.

'Fine,' said Jack.

The two boys entered the house, went up the stairs and entered the boy's room. Tim went into the closet saying, 'Start the timer now, and closed the door behind him.

Ten minutes went by and everything was okay, then Tim heard scratching noises on the back of the closet and started to feel something scraping his leg. Feeling something running down the back of his leg, he screamed and ran outside, followed by his friend. He told his friends what happened and after five minutes he passed out from lack of blood. He went to hospital and was fine after a few days.

All of the five boys knew what happened and knew the story was true. They will never forget what happened that day.

Sian Lloyd (11)

The Boy With The Blue Eyes

The boy with the blue eyes
His hair is black and is short.
The boy with blue eyes,
Is tall and at the same time short.
The boy with blue eyes
Has a face like silk
But ...

The boy with blue eyes
Sits by himself.
The boy with blue eyes
Sits at the back.
The boy with blue eyes never talks
But ...

The boy with blue eyes
Has no friends.
The boy with blue eyes
Is never rude.
The boy with the blue eyes
In fact
That the boy with the blue eyes is the perfect pupil at the school.
But ...

The boy with the blue eyes has
An expression like ice,
Hands are cold to the bone,
Clothes that smell like old moss
But ...

Why would this student of mine
The one with eyes so blue like a clear summer's sky?

Please do not think ill of him
Take pity on this boy
For if you do not
Those eyes
That boy with the blue eyes
Shall be the last thing you ever see!

Regan Mulcahy (13)

Full Moon

He waited. He watched.
Unknown. Unseen.

It was pitch-black outside; the moon long ago had risen to the highest point in the sky. It was a full moon. There were no stars, just a vast black ocean, stretching out as far as the eye could see. An owl hooted somewhere in the distance.

The man stopped abruptly and turned around. His large round eyes scanned the darkness. His heart beat faster. His watch read three minutes to midnight. He composed himself quickly, and hurried on through the empty street. He reached his house. The man didn't know why, but when the saw the house, something about it made the hairs on the back of his neck stand up. He had an odd feeling about it.

One minute to midnight. In eagerness to get out of the darkness, he took out his keys and hurriedly jammed them into the lock. He began climbing the stairs slowly, unwillingly. He realised he was scared. Thirty seconds. He did not want to go in his room, he was wary. He didn't get a choice. The door swung noisily open though the man's arms hadn't left his side. He was waiting of course.

At last, the time had come. Five seconds. The man screamed shrilly, panic erupting inside him. The whole house was ringing with the sound of the piercing scream.

One second. The man fell to the floor, eyes wide.

Midnight.

The man was no longer human.

Jessica Owen (13)

Untitled

As she turned the corner she screamed. She had known he was going to be there, he had been round every other corner. She turned and ran towards the park but he was close behind her. He grabbed her hair, pulling her down to the ground; she was forced to see his face again. The yellowing dead skin and red scars running across his face from where she'd fought him off last night. He healed quickly; she had killed him so many times. Hacked him apart, bled him to death, shot him … but the wounds would just heal and he'd come back the next night.

She knew what she had to do now. She had learnt from every night and slowly realised exactly what she would have to do. She just had to lay there and die in his arms. She had once loved him but now he would only leave her alone when she was dead. She could not endure his torture anymore. She would die in her dead lover's arms tonight.

Jessica Deacon (13)

The House That Everyone Talks About

That's where it all took place. The memory of it will always be near me, goading me, whispering its malice. It was I who witnessed it happen. It is I who bears the vivid images to this day.

People tell the lie of the haunted house because they do not know any better. She was my sister and that was no accident and that night no joke. When I first heard her screaming, I ignored her pitiful cries - I didn't think it was anything more than a pathetic call for attention. When the shrieking, the sobbing, the heart-wrenching sobs didn't stop, I went to investigate.

She was there on a chair in the middle of the room, writhing around madly, with tears streaming down her cheeks. I couldn't understand why she wouldn't get up, but she shouted something about the bonds of a spirit and that I must get out.

I couldn't understand. I was at loss for what to do! I told her to stop messing but she continued to flail about crazily and she began tearing at her scalp. Then there were the clumps of hair that fell to the floor, matted with blood. Oh, the blood that splurged from freshly-made cuts. Where the cuts came from, I didn't know and I didn't know how and I didn't understand. And with that final breath, she breathed her last and all I am left with are memories of the past.

Isabelle Kenyon (14)

Spooked

It was a Monday night. All was sound. Then I noticed the full moon that shone above me. A howl came from the bushes and the sound of rustling surrounded me. A slurp of blood found its way to my ears. When I turned around ready to run I found a dog standing there. My God!

I ran home to find my mum dead on the floor. As I fell I saw a blood-sucking monster and his sidekick wolf beside him.

10 years later …
My mum was running around collecting blood and capturing humans for their tea. They were a happy couple together after the incident. Someone knocked on the door in the middle of the forest. The man said there was going to be a war, vampire against humans.

The next thing I knew I was in vampire court, ready to go to war …

Jasmine Hadley (11)

The Haunted Hotel

It was Halloween. The scary sisters (that's us) finished trick or treating. We had a reputation for being the scariest in town and we didn't fail to impress this year. We dared each other to go into The Francis - a creepy, derelict, old hotel.

'Rumour has it, it's haunted!' Mel smiled.

'What we waiting for then?' I laughed.

'Locked,' Kelly stated, pushing the gates.

Mel climbed over the top. Kelly looked at me; I shrugged, climbing after her. We stood in front of the door, quiet, awed by the size of it. I gulped. My hands were sweating, my heart thudding fast. The door slowly swung open. I looked at my friends - the scary sisters right? Wrong - at that moment in time we were the scared sisters.

'C-come on then,' I stammered. I slowly walked through the door into the dank, dark, musty house, Kelly and Mel following nervously. Switching on my torch, the door shut with a bang.

'Just the window,' I said, hoping more than believing it was true.

Suddenly something shoved me, I dropped my torch, resulting in pitch blackness.

'Argh!' I screamed. 'Kelly? Mel?' I screamed again. There was a blood-curdling cry, soft footsteps walking away. 'Mel? Kelly?' I said panicking.

'I'm here,' Mel replied, feeling her way towards me. We hugged, then let go.

'Where's Kelly?' I said hysterically.

Silence.

'Mel?' I said worried.

Silence.

Suddenly, someone or something grabbed me. I tried screaming but I was so petrified nothing came out. Then … silence.

Lisa Head (13)

Lost Soldier

Shaking from the cold, Private Conner Brimply stood alone in the night. Mud walls to his front and back, Conner listened for any noise of enemy movement. Nothing. Just the silence.

But instead of bringing comfort to Conner, the silence seemed sinister, menacing, intimidating. Conner hated living on the Western Front; hated living with what he had come to know as 'doomed men' but who everyone else called 'the lads'. Everyone else. That was the problem; Conner just wasn't like *everyone else*. He was … different.

Then, Conner heard the screaming. A guttural noise, like an animal coming to a cruel end, rent the air. Conner jumped, tripping over his feet and falling flat on his back.

Suddenly, a green mist appeared. Ugly, but strangely elegant, the fog materialised out of the night air as suddenly as a bird bursting from a bush. Then came the shouting. Shadows appeared out of the mist, clearly men dressed in full combat gear. They rushed towards a hunched, moaning shape curled on the floor a few feet away from Conner.

All of a sudden, the shadows moved away and the hunched shape leapt up and ran towards Conner. Before Conner could do anything, a hideous face leered out of the darkness. Its mouth was all froth and its eyes burnt red with pain. The skin was pale, burned and cracked. The thing, whatever it was, was choking, screaming, begging for help.

Conner fainted as the gas closed in around him, smothering in its choking grip …

Elliot Elstob (15)

The Attic

It was the day Caitlin was moving house. She was so excited but in a way sad because she had lived in that house for eight years. But the new house was so big and her room was indescribably big. The moving truck had just arrived and was packing up. It didn't take them long, only two hours.

They were on their way to the new house, it didn't take that long because it was only a couple of miles away but when they got there she was so excited to start unpacking.

About six hours later it was time to go to bed. She said to herself, 'I will finish unpacking tomorrow.' Her mum came in and said goodnight.

She woke up at midnight to the sound of footsteps, she didn't realise where they were coming from so she went outside.

'Mum, is that you going to the toilet?' she cried. No reply so she went back to bed. Then she realised where they were coming from, they were coming from the attic. She was scared so she cuddled up with teddy, then she heard a *thump!* She was really scared now, her heart was beating out of her chest and her hands were trembling. Then she heard *drip, drip*.

She screamed! It was blood dripping from the attic. Then she heard footsteps again then the attic door opened …

'Has anyone got any ketchup?' a figure cried. Poor Caitlin thought there had been a murder but it was only someone wanting ketchup for a hot dog.

Katrina Larsen-Kittle (11)

Jimmy And The Creaks

Jimmy got a very eerie feeling. He was watching TV downstairs. Creaks appeared from upstairs. His mum said boldly that it was time for bed. He had to go upstairs.

Jimmy crept up the stairs, heart pounding and stood still. Larger creaks now emerged. He ran into the bathroom and locked the door. Jimmy placed the washing basket in front of the door. Now he dared himself to get into the shower. Now stressed, he turned on the shower, jumped in while it was freezing and turned it straight off.

The door rattled.

He shivered and started hyperventilating. Jimmy tried to forget all about it. He couldn't. While cautiously drying himself and getting his pyjamas on, no creaks were heard. He moved the washing basket back. The lights went off. Jimmy screamed then the door burst open …

Lee Sutton (13)

Zashiki Walashi

One day after school my girls' group went to Holland garden to play. There were ten of us and what we did was sit around and told spooky stories. We told them because it was Halloween day.

Finally it was my turn and I told a Japanese folk tale story called Zashiki Walashi. The story was about ten children who were playing in a big manor house (a living room), they were all happily playing.

A few hours later their mums came to pick their children up. One of the kids counted them all and there were eleven of them, they were all common faces, none of them knew who the new one was and the doors were all closed, none of them had gone in or out.

When I finished, all my friends had terrified faces.

My friend Maya mumbled, 'Let's play 'it'.' We all agreed.

We played for ten minutes and then our mum started shouting, 'We are going home!'

We quickly counted how many of us there were and there were eleven! We didn't know who the new one was and we looked each other.

We shouted at the top of our voices, 'Zashiki Walashi!' We screamed and ran away.

Hibiki-Hitomi Sakuta (8)

The Sofa Ghost

It was a dark and stormy night in Oaklington and Mrs Reeves had just put all her children to bed and was watching a programme. She had just sat down on the royal red sofa when she heard baby Danielle screaming on the baby monitor so she rushed upstairs to see what was happening.

She went into Danielle's room which she shared with another baby girl, Clara and two-year-old girl Martha. To her astonishment, Danielle, Clara and Martha weren't there.

She called their names, 'Danielle, Clara, Martha, where are you?' She ran into all the other children's rooms and to her pleasure they were all in eleven-year-old Jack's room reading stories.

Mrs Reeves walked down all the stairs and went back to her TV programme.

Mrs Reeves had been watching the telly for about ten minutes when she looked over to the window and saw a figure, half a figure, looking at her so she walked over and shut the curtains. She walked back over to the sofa, her heels tapping on the hardwood floor. She turned round anxiously to see if the figure *was* still there and to her amazement the figure *was* still there. She suddenly realised that the figure wasn't looking through the window but it was standing right next to the sofa and even worse, she had walked through it!

From now Mrs Reeves will sit in the middle of the sofa!

Josie Bristow-Booker (9)

The Nightmare

The figures ran riot. Billy was sitting in the corner weeping. Barbie destroyed his bed, Action Man smashed his mirror then threw the remains at him, Ken squirted toothpaste all over his bedroom, Danger Mouse was just staring while Snow White was escaping through the window.

The next morning, as Billy went to school, he was shouting, 'Hey Toby, wait up. I need to tell you something.' He was as eager as a hungry eagle. But every time he thought of the night before he had a flashback and heard screaming just like a nightmare.

His friends laughed as he told them the story. *Is it me or are they staring at me?* he thought. He walked off.

He waited until someone walked past, he told them the story but got the same reaction as the other people he had told. He slumped home.

As he got in he heard whispering from upstairs. He crept up and walked into his bedroom. Silence. 'Hello?' Still silence. 'Anyone here?' …

'I've been expecting you.' The door slammed shut.

Morgan Rusted (12)

Risk

The only house left on the street, right at the end, beside a dead tree with no leaves. Many tales and stories have been made but who knows the truth?

Death was what the house was made of. Danger on every step. Waiting for someone to end his *thirst!* All I could see was nothing. I didn't even dare to take a breath, not letting anyone feel or hear my presence. Heart pounding, head bursting off, horrendously bad flashbacks like I was linked to this house in a way. I felt *death* all over me. I was horrified and totally devastated inside. I knew I was going to be killed unmercifully.

Standing by the wall, feeling no use of having two eyes which didn't enable me to look through the dominating darkness throughout the house. For the last time I tried to find those wonderful memories hidden right into beautiful parts of my brain but the only thought that came across was *death*.

Suddenly a white figure came visible to my eyes. It was coming after me. It was coming after me. What should I do? I ran towards the only light I could see coming through a small crack in the wall. It seemed to be the only hope now but it disappeared! I don't know where! I don't know how! I fainted!

Was I left dead or alive? Still a mystery and will remain one.

Usman Irfan (14)

Sunset

Chloe hid underneath the duvet and shivered. Every time she fell asleep she had the dream, the same dream, always the same dream.

It began beautifully. She would watch the sun setting and listen to the birds singing their evening song. Then it would go cold and everything would slow down. In a dream you can never scream but Chloe tried very hard to. She could feel it welling up in her throat but nothing came out.

The birds would stop singing, as if they knew something was about to happen and Chloe would turn her gaze to the sky. Surely the sun hadn't been that big five minutes ago? And surely the sky hadn't been that red?

She would watch as the sun would swell up and turn completely red. It doubled, tripled and quadrupled in size in what could have been seconds or years to Chloe. The nearby trees caught fire, scattering birds and knocking Chloe out of her sunshock, but she couldn't think of anything logical to do so she sat down again and watched the scene unfold. The last thing she would see would be fire.

Then Chloe woke up ... and this time she could scream.

Daniel Penney-Gallagher (11)

The Lady In White

Ellie looked out of the steamed up window. There!
'Yes, it's her, the one that I saw when I was younger. So don't follow her!' Mum said, looking away in disgust.

'Why don't we follow her?' Ellie asked.

'When I was a child, children would go missing out on the moors. It was the lady, they would follow her out so far that they couldn't find their way back and they were never seen again. It was like following a rainbow; you could never find the end of the trail until it was too late,' Mum explained.

That night Ellie dreamt about the lady. She was dressed in a white dress, stained with age. Ellie ran across the cold windy moors. Suddenly the woman turned around, she stared at Ellie with cold, dark eyes.

'Help! She's here, she's ... she's gone.' Ellie looked around her, nothing. The woman with her cold eyes and torn dress had gone.

'Darling, why are you outside? You'll catch a death, here, put my coat on and explain on the way inside.' Mum put her arms around Ellie's shoulders.

'I dreamt that the woman was taking me away but I resisted, when she turned around, I saw her eyes. It was so horrible.' Ellie was now shaking, partly of fear, partly of chill.

'Well, let's get you inside and warm. I may let you sleep in my room, eh?' Mum always managed to cheer her up one way or another.

Elizabeth Rose Facer (13)

The Death Of Riley Stewart

Tyler backed to the corner of the empty room. The black-hooded figure surged closer. 'Get away from me freak!' Tyler yelled.

Instead the strange figure cocked its head and whispered, 'No!' It raised a shovel … *bang!* Tyler blacked out.

He opened his eyes and blinked hard with disbelief. 'Why am I outside? Why is there oil all over me?' The sky was purple. The air was cold. The clouds were grey and foggy. *Creak!* He turned quickly. It was just the wind. 'Argh!' Tyler shrieked. It was there, right in front of his face.

'Hello Tyler, remember me?' It was Riley, Riley Stewart. 'Long time no see, I wonder why?' she cackled.

Before Tyler could answer she slowly took off her hood. Tyler gasped in shock, 'No!' He backed away. Her flesh was pink and lumpy. Riley's eyes were yellow and sharp. She had no nose, her ears were torn and the side of her face was scarred.

'You're not going anywhere,' she chuckled and lit a match. 'See you in Hell,' she hissed.

Subah Sabur (12)

Midnight Visit

A loud buzzing rang in my head. It was an incessant, annoying buzzing. But what was it? I tried to open my eyes, but tiredness washed over me. My gut feeling told me that I had to wake up. *Come on Jay*, I thought to myself, slowly forcing my eyes open.

The instant my eyes were open the buzzing came to a sudden halt and I was left staring into nothingness. All the weariness I'd felt earlier had vanished. I tilted my head towards the Bambi digital clock I've had since I was eight, which usually sits on my bedside table. But no red digits jumped at me. I reached out, feeling for it but all my hand touched was cold air. I winced as the icy breeze sliced through my hand like a knife. Was that even possible? At that exact moment, I heard an uncanny crackling laugh from the corner of my bedroom.

'Jay-Jay, Jay-Jay,' a voice croaked, 'I know you're there Jay-Jay.'

This was definitely a …

'This is not a dream Jay-Jay,' the voice screeched abruptly, reading my thoughts absolutely. All of a sudden, a white haze entered my vision and a deafening sound shrilled in my ear. I couldn't bear it, it was killing me.

'Who are you?' I yelled, trying not to sound as scared as I felt. But no reply came, a dark eeriness enveloped me and the frosty cold I'd felt before wrapped around me.

'Welcome, Jay-Jay,' whispered my ghost, my future.

Nadia Madoui (13)

Curse

At first it seemed gentle and cute; as I crept closer I could hear it weeping. The shadows were covering its face. The figure was misty and human-like, by now it was staring at the floor. You could tell its head was tilted downwards.

'Are you okay?' I timidly asked.

No reply.

Its head raised slowly, it was a girl - a ghost girl! She was weeping; white splashes fell to the floor and slowly faded away.

'Who are you?' I asked.

'Nobody, a dead nobody!' she cried.

'Don't be frightened, I want to help.' I replied.

'I'm sure you cannot, just leave me be!' she shouted.

She turned around - half of her head was missing, her brain was eaten away. The shock made me feel sick, I felt like I was about to spew my guts up all over her. A shiver ran through my spine.

'You poor girl!' I said sympathetically.

'I had a tragic accident and I died, now leave or you will behold the powerful curse.' She wept.

I ran as far and as fast as my feet could carry me through the iron gates of Tumbridge Manor. I had a throbbing migraine; I fell to the floor in pain ...

Maisie Dixon (11)

Mystery Of The Long Grass

He entered the house; slowly a thick fog came flowing out of the door. He crept over to the kitchen but the door was locked. The man lingered over to the back door, it creaked open. The grass was 10 foot tall. He wandered around in the back garden … no one was there.

The old man shuffled up the ancient stairs, they creaked loudly. He walked into the primitive back room and looked out of the window. There was a man; he was in the garden cutting the 10 foot grass. Who was he? How did he get in?

The old man who stared out of the window slowly crept down the stairs. He tippy toed over to the back door when the kitchen's door lock clicked undone. What could this be?

The man walked into the kitchen but there was no one there. He turned around and shuffled over to the back door. The once 10 foot tall grass was now 1 foot!

Arnold Lincoln (12)

The Unknown

Josh took one look behind him as he stepped into the threshold of the house. For years it had been rumoured to be haunted by an old man who had fallen down the stairs to his death and until now, Josh hadn't believed a word of it. His friends had dared him to come down and he desperately wished he had refused now as he took in the mildewed floorboards and peeling wallpaper. The darkness was thick and oppressive, intoxicating even, and it was difficult to breathe. Josh gingerly stepped forward and the floorboard groaned in protest but he ignored it. There was a slither of light coming from a window and outside, the moon could be seen, a lonesome orb, floating in a ghostly luminescence.

A floorboard creaked upstairs and something fell over and smashed. Josh's head turned towards the sound and he felt the hairs on the back of his neck stand on end. A cool breeze swept across the boy's face and the room appeared to become even darker. Then the single candle that Josh held, flickered and then faded into a ghostly swirl of smoke which spiralled towards the ceiling like an angelic ballerina. Josh panicked and rushed for the door.

He felt cool night air rush against his face and he ran down the path straight into his friends, who had been waiting for him.

'So?' they asked. 'Is it really haunted?'

'Yes,' Josh replied. 'But the thing that haunts that place is not something one can hear, see or touch. No, the thing that haunts that place is not a ghost or monster; it is so much more than that. That house is haunted purely by fear!'

Blythe Rachael Britz (12)

The Porcelain Cup

Carrie flashed the barcode under the scanner. *Come on,* she thought, *work.* The customer snorted impatiently, waiting for the porcelain teacup to come through. Yet, as always, when time is tight and patience tighter, the barcode simply wouldn't work.

After glancing anxiously around the empty supermarket Carrie muttered, 'Gimme a sec, I need a new one … we're short staffed tonight.'

As she hurried off through cool, lonely aisles, Carrie thought this wasn't strictly true, there were staff, they were just outside holding off the protesters. The town of Daneford was a quiet pocket of untouched tradition - or so it had been, before FreshBuy, the nation's fastest growing supermarket, foolishly decided to open a new branch here - and on a heritage site no less! To pacify the angry locals her managers had brought in a range of cups patterned in local designs - but not even the refrigerator aisle could cool the burning fury of these protesters.

Carrie, at last, reached the back aisle and roughly snatched at the nearest cup. Her fingers missed and it fell sharply to the floor and shattered. At once, all the other cups began to shake. Stumbling away, Carrie ran out into the store but as her eyes racked the shelves around her, all that could be sensed was rotting food, soggy cardboard boxes, fruit crawling with maggots, meat long turned black with mould.

And roughly, a scarred, croaky voice, 'Not welcome!'

The lights flickered.

The food returned, clean, fresh and ready to buy.

Rachel Tookey (17)

Miss

It all happened on a clear Tuesday evening. It was the 31st of October, Halloween night. Tommy, his twin, Natasha, and a few of their mates were trick or treating round Petersburg.

'Come on, let's get Old Man Richmond's house,' yelled Elfie, Tommy's best friend.

The kids walked up the hill, round the bend then down the road till they were outside Old Man Richmond's house.

K-Leigh, the youngest of the group, was a little more hesitant about the idea. 'M-maybe we s-shouldn't d-do this,' K-Leigh stuttered, backing out.

'Don't care, we got here, we are not backing down now,' called out Tommy.

The boys ran through the creaking gate up to the icy-covered house and looked back to Natasha and K-Leigh.

'Be careful, please be careful,' cried Natasha.

'We'll be fine, stop worrying,' yelled out Elfie before bravely knocking on the metal door that hung over their heads.

After a few seconds the boys turned to walk back.

'See, nothing to worry about,' stated Tommy when suddenly the door opened with a screech.

'Uhhh, we s-should g-go now,' started Natasha whilst K-Leigh nodded in the background.

All of a sudden the shadow of Old Man Richmond appeared and the boys disappeared.

'W-where are we?' cried Tommy and Elfie panicking in the darkness.

'This will teach you to spy on me, won't it?' yelled Old Man Richmond from a distance.

'Yes, yes, we promise not to spy,' squeaked the boys, practically in tears.

Suddenly they were back outside, 'Let's go home girls.'

Aimeé Louisa Parris (12)

The Shadow

They sat there, cold and wet. The shadow was circling them. Under the canopy of the bush seemed like the safest place to be but nowhere was safe. It continued, round and round and round. They breathed slowly in and out, in and out.

Suddenly there was a scream that pierced that chilled air. It came from behind them. They sat completely frozen but the shadow didn't stop. Nobody knew what it was. Maybe it was a vampire coming to suck out their souls. Maybe it was a werewolf coming to rip them to shreds like a piece of raw meat. Maybe?

The glittering light of the moon shone on the house ahead of them. If they could just make it up the bending drive then maybe they'd be safe. Another scream, except this time it came from above. Again the shadow never stopped, it got faster like a great white shark circling its prey. They could hear whispers. They were getting closer. Their eyes didn't move from the shadow. It came to an abrupt stop then faded away. *Is it safe?* they asked themselves as the minutes dragged on. They daren't speak, they daren't move.

Another scream, but somehow this one was different, it was one of them. A finger pointed to the other side of the bush. There it was, just hanging there. A hand, a cold blue hand. Motionless, the children stared. It was dead, they were sure of that … or were they?

Alice Shaw (12)

Next ...

'Rain falls
*It don't touch the ground
I can recall an empty house ...'*

That's exactly how I felt; I wasn't sure what exactly did happen that day but the impact of the event was still here.

I looked around my empty room, tears springing to my eyes, as I finally remembered what happened, after a week of it happening.

It was a rainy day, matching my mood. My friend and I had got into an argument, her storming out of the hours we shared after she stormed out. I sighed and plugged in my black iPod to a random song, Screamo playing as I sighed again.

I got up and went out for a walk; the rain started pelting my skin making me calm once more. The air held a mysteriously sinister atmosphere. I tried ignoring it with my music on full blast.

Suddenly I heard a shriek from my right, the road was clear, not a single person in sight. I made up my mind and ran in the direction of the shriek. Another noise came, this time at a wrenching sound, which made my stomach churn. I ran faster, around the corner. What I saw was so ... so gruesome ...

A girl, she was lying on the ground, her stomach sliced open and her organs missing. I looked away, disgusted.

'You're next,' a voice whispered. A chill went up my spine, making me cold to the core. I whipped my head around, seeing no one there.

Ruhama Gill (12)

Hide And Kill

'Wake up or you are going to be late,' bellowed Sam.

'OK coming,' I screamed. Me and Sam were going to a trip for Halloween. They say it is a haunted house but I know they are lying. (I do not believe in that junk.)

'Come on,' shouted Sam.

We left the house, we went to school. Only ten people can go in at a time so the first ten went in and came out okay. Then me, Sam, Mark, Toni, John, Joanna, Leon, Richard, Vanessa and Carla went in.

When we stepped into the house I saw a shadow swaying. I ran to the door to get out. I was terrified. Before I could get halfway to the door it shut. Everybody ran to the door and started banging.

'Let me out!' Toni, Joanna and John had disappeared into mid-air! My mouth turned to an O shape.

I ran to Sam and said, 'Do not leave me please.' I blinked and she had disappeared.

There was only me, Mark, Leon, Richard, Vanessa and Carla left. (I think it is a haunted house with ghosts and stuff.)

We all ran upstairs. Carla and Vanessa went missing! There were only four people left. Who could be doing this?

Richard and Leon went off without us. We heard a scream.

When I got there Mark was not behind me. I was walking around the house and I saw Joanna and Sam with a fog around them. I ran to them, I was halfway when they turned into ghosts!

I turned around and opened the door, I was free or was I? I was attacked from the back and …

Vanessa Ezeugwa (12)

Valentine

Night was beginning to fall. The clouds moved, closing in on one another. The light scurried up the walls of the ancient buildings, leaving the open-mouthed gargoyles in the deep shadows. Lucinda hurried down the damp street, the trees shook violently behind her. Rain was beginning to trickle down, Lucinda ran to shelter herself from the harshness of the weather which was growing ferocious. Lightning shrieked, illuminating the gargoyles' grotesque faces especially their sharp-pointed teeth, edging outwards.

Lucinda closed her eyes in fear but all that flashed behind them was the book cover of Valentine, the scariest book she had ever read. It was the cover which first grabbed her attention at the library. A black wilted rose with drops of blood on it. Her train of thought was lost as gusts of wind rattled the bus stop and sent shivers up Lucinda's back. No, she definitely shouldn't have read it, it was making her feel paranoid. She decided to walk home and not wait for the next bus.

Lucinda was halfway down the street when she realised she heard something behind her. *Crunch.* She turned, startled to find a black wilted rose dripping with blood. Her heartbeat accelerated. A dark figure appeared out of the shadows. He drew nearer, she ran but then he was in front of her. The strange figure opened his mouth. It was black and hollow as death. His mouth stretched open at an unnatural length, swallowing her into the gates of Hell.

Katrina Jan (16)

The Funfair - Or Not!

We all love going to the funfair - don't we? There was a boy called Jack and he loved funfairs until one sunny day he decided to go to the funfair with his mum and dad.

The funfair was still open for another half an hour and Jack still had £2.50 left which was burning a hole in his pocket. Then suddenly there was a place that caught his eye - The Magic Hall of Mirrors. He was the only one in there, which was a privilege for Jack because there had been a massive queue for everything else. He was looking at all the mirrors and then suddenly he heard a laugh, it wasn't just an ordinary laugh - it was freaky. Jack just thought it was a cool sound effect.

Jack gasped. There in the mirror was a clown but the scary thing about it was that if he turned around it wasn't there. It had a really scary smile painted on its face. It had a horrible laugh.

Then suddenly the clown's hand popped out of the mirror and it was holding a balloon. Jack took the balloon and then he vanished! He was flying down a deep hole.

Boom! He hit the ground and found himself on his bedroom floor, as if it was all a dream and he had fallen off his bed.

Rowan Smith (11)

The Lonely Hospital

There was a dark mist in the air, tall trees stood like ladders holding a million crows on each step. A chalky, black shrub stood in a miniature clearing with a hand reaching out to grab something, pointing at something. Silence stood and whispery echoes bounced around the dead forest.

Screams arose from the blue misty darkness, it sounded like the dead shriek of horror, so close yet unreal. In response thunderous squawks filled the air as flapping birds left the scene. Silence came back around as the smell of ashes overwhelmed the few living souls around.

From the corner of an eye something moved, the hand-shaped branch stretched its fingers out and reached for something. I felt it grab hold of my heart and it yanked. Everything became a blur as I fell towards the ground.

Rubbing my eyes I awoke with a world spinning before me. I sat up, taking in my surroundings. I figured that I was in an old tatty hospital. Just at that moment a nurse wandered by, her bones rattled. With maggots instead of eyes the creature still had a small amount of flesh on her right side but was mostly bone. Rotten but cheerful, the nurse turned round to stare at me, maggots staring too. Her right side gave out a mouldy smile before she continued on her way. Was I dreaming or was this really a hospital of the dead?

Freya Christina Smith (11)

Scratchings On The Wall

It was when we had just moved to Devon when my life was scarred. When the screaming started and when the noises got louder I thought it was just our old house. We used to hear crying babies, screaming women and laughing men. It was like torture listening to people being literally tortured but we never linked it to that masterpiece on the wall.

This is my story and I hope you're not reading it alone. When we lived in Birmingham we used to hear screaming, crying and footsteps pacing up and down our staircase. We figured it was just the house so we moved, simple as.

But the first night me and my little sister, Lottie, heard a knock on our door. We opened it and as usual there was nothing there and then when we got into the bed there was a dark black figure looming over us like willow trees. We both tried to scream but it was like we couldn't.

When we told our parents they didn't believe us and we had to sleep in that room again. Lottie managed to sleep in my arms but I simply couldn't. When I lay down there were scratching noises on the bed. Lottie heard it too. We could have sword it said, 'Lily' but we couldn't be sure.

So the next morning we got up and searched the house. We stupidly went into the attic and saw the dark figure looming over a painting of a girl. Was this the Lily he was talking about?

We looked and saw a figure inside the painting, behind the girl. It was him - the figure. I knew it was and I burned it. And after that it was gone and I'm damn glad!

Jodie Marsden (12)

Horror Day

One day I was in my grandmother's house in the middle of the country. When I entered the house it was all dark and I heard a person moving things in the basement. I got into the basement and saw it was a woman with a knife in her hand. It was really dark so I couldn't see very well. I imagined it was a thief.

Then, she moved close to me and she touched my arms. I was very nervous.

Then she turned on the light and it was my grandmother cutting meat there because the kitchen was dirty and she had a beautiful table in her basement. It was a horror day! Never in my life will I enter this house alone!

Micaela Arroyo Zugarramurdi (14)

Blessing: The Nightmare

It was a dry day; the scorching heat glazed all vision, midday in Mumbai. A sudden uproar sprouted from the Eastern district, the children ran in excitement. Their tongues and hands reached for the rain, a Municipal water pipe had burst. The atmosphere was frantic and energised. Flashing light from their skin, moisture rejuvenated their dried out hands and feet as the curse sang over their bones. The men and women butting in with pots, tins, buckets and pans came to a halt, the rush died out. Their silence made way for the screams and taunts that filled the air, the beasty god screeched in agony.

The children of the dead woke up, freed from the water, resurrected in the local children's bodies. Their fangs dug into the terrified congregation. Their bodies turned pale orange, their eyes darkened, into the colour of the abyss. Wings sprouted from their backs, claws grew. Their nails grew larger, arms and legs multiplied in size, the children lifted off into the sky circled around the community, dived down, clutched and ate. Ripping off their tendons, biting off their heads, blood squirted everywhere. The skies turned sharp yellow, into a dark black.

All went faint, a light glistened through the sky's epicentre, the screeching, screaming and yelling faded. An earthquake shook the ground, it went on and on …

'Mary! Mary! For Heaven's sake wake up, look, you are sweating!' Mary's mother said aggravated. She woke Mary violently with concern and tears filling her eyes.

Thandiwe Tafireyi (17)

The Terror Seeker

L ike the shadow of a tree on your bedroom wall, that you're sure is something terrible trying to reach you, the hand reached out towards Liz. Its ghostly fingers curling around her like a boa constrictor, squeezing the precious life out of its prey. Liz looked at me, her blue eyes pleading with me to help her, pleading with me to save her but I couldn't. If I did I would be sure to face the same horrifying fate as her. I didn't want to watch but my eyes were glued to the nightmarish scene before me. I watched as Liz opened her mouth to scream, even though there was no one to hear her - no one but me, but before she could utter a sound the shadowy fingers covered her mouth - silencing her forever.

I had to get out. The creature had stolen the life of the rest of the people on this doomed school trip. That's what it did - it fed on their terror, their hatred. It sucked their feelings out of them. It enclosed its victims in its blackness till they were gone, swallowed up by its dark mass. Their souls trapped forever inside of it. I was the only one left; it was only a matter of time before it sensed my fear my hopelessness and moved in to finish me off like it had the others. I did the only thing I could think of ... I ran.

Serena Arthur (12)

Alleyway

There's one thing that I've always wondered about. If you leave someone to die or you drive them to it, should it rest on your conscience and if so for how long? Does it just go away? Because for me it did. I left a person to die and I felt nothing afterwards. So does it make me a killer?

Walking through the alleyway in the pitch-black, it was destined for something to happen. I mean you get told all these stories of 'bad men' hiding in dark places preying on young, innocent girls who were out late by themselves. However it wasn't me who was attacked. Yet.

So as I made my way home in the dark, I tripped and landed flat on my face.

'Ouch!' With my palms to wet ground, I jumped quickly to my feet and as I went to wipe my hand across my face I noticed blood on my hands. But wait, my face had taken in all the impact, not my hands. This meant, it wasn't my blood!

I heard the crunching of wet stones. As I turned, all I wished was, *why did I have to find this?* I hadn't tripped over my own feet this time; I had tripped over a bloodied corpse. So much for being in a safe place, thanks Mum. Instead of screaming like a normal person I just stood there. Then I saw the body move but what could I do?

Mandeep Bal (16)

Floored

A once typical boy, Reuben, lived in a run-down area 22 miles from Texas. He was one of the five children left in Clanton after the bombings and spent most of his time exploring the town's abandoned buildings with his best friend, Lee. Normally they were never allowed past the old water tower but the adults were out of town and not much was normal about their lives now.

They stepped through the rotting wooden gates into the once buzzing streets. Four years ago a bomber plane flew over Texas, when all the townsfolk thought it had run out of ammunition it flew towards their little town and dropped its last incendiary bomb over the western edge of town leaving it reduced to a wreckage and 300 dead. Only one house stood strong. It belonged to a recluse, the former mayor, Ray Robinson. He was thought to have perished on that fateful night.

They stepped up the death black steps; the door was broken like someone had been trying to get out. Reuben felt chilled and suddenly realised Lee was gone. He wrenched open the burnt doors only to find himself alone in a giant empty room. All of a sudden he heard the door slam shut behind him and all traces of light vanished. His heart was pounding as he crept up the stairs into a long narrow hallway and his only thought was to escape. Then the truth hit him and suddenly so did the floor …

Thomas Taylor (12)

The Entity

Thousands of voices spoke in my brain whispering, *why?* The plain white walls seemed to close in on me. These walls told stories of broken hearts and wished upon dreams that were never to be seen again. The familiar smell of some sort of distasteful medication or silky pungent fragrance of bleach lingered through the air, suffocating me.

I was starting to think I was stuck in the room for any longer, not only will I lose my sense of smell, I might start losing my mind too. My face went slack, mouth slightly open, body unmoving and colour draining from my face as I stared wide-eyed at something no one else could see. I just froze up to a point where I could hardly breathe but when shock began to melt away, everything returned to me slowly. Sweat slowly trickled down my steamy, puffy face.

As my eyes began to focus clearer I noticed the black figure appear again. Thick, navy blue veins swelled through her chalky, wax paper skin. Her beady-black eyes glared with the nothingness from where she came, a lost memory, no known value. Feathers of dark hair dangled from her bony skull, the strands resembled the dead of night. I looked at her, transfixed by her presence; she turned and pierced me with her gleaming emerald stare. Her eyes seemed to bore into the depths of my soul. There was no question that she was real or not. I wanted to run out of here, anywhere.

Rabiat Umar (13)

Something Ghostly Is Going On In Lancaster

Have you ever heard of a pirate called Captain Peter Capbird? He was a lazy old man who didn't like clever pirates at all. He never told or showed anyone the map he had or what it was like or where it led to. He was famous for fantastic cooking, that was a pretty silly thing to be famous for in those times. But it did happen.

Then one night a crew member came into his bedroom and killed him by stabbing him seven times in the chest. But no one knew that two people called Jacob and Becky were going to find out!

One dark cold night when the graveyard was black and foggy, something strange happened, something ghostly. Captain Peter Capbird came back in the form of a ghost. He haunted everywhere to find his map that he had for the whole of his life. He never let anyone see it but one of his crew found the map and buried it at the seaside but what seaside? He searched everywhere to find it.

Then one night Jacob and Becky found it after they dug down 60 feet. They took it back to their lab to see where it came from and whose it was.

Captain Peter Capbird had a fantastic sense of smell, from his cooking of course, and smelt his map. As quick as a flash he went to where his map was and tried to pick up but he couldn't. As Jacob could see ghosts he made a machine that could turn ghosts back to real people.

Captain Peter Capbird turned back and snatched the lamp off the table and ran as fast as he could, he jumped on his ship and went to the location … but the treasure had gone!

Stephanie Louise Sargent (9)

The Haunted Darkness

I ran and ran, my heart pounding, my feet thundering on the rough forest floor. The dense dark forest rushed past me in a blur. The forest we had been warned about.

The cold air left me breathless. I stopped momentarily, stood still and listened. Where was Joe? I could see no sign of him and terror gripped me as I realised I was alone. I ran again, directionless, branches scratching my cheeks, tree roots trying to trip me. Then I heard it, the evil whisper on the wind. 'Death,' it said and then again, 'Death.' Faster I ran; sweat pouring into my eyes wide with fear.

Out of nowhere came an ear-piercing scream, striking the air like a lightning bolt. I froze and as I raised my hands to cover my ears, I saw it. A misty shadow passed through me, causing me to shudder. As it span me into a dizzy whir, I closed my eyes longing for it to stop. Then again, 'Death,' the wind whispered. Where was Joe?

A single beam of moonlight lit the forest floor like a narrow path ahead of me. I staggered along it, still dizzy, fumbling my way through the moving forest. Another heart-stopping scream made me quicken my pace. I was desperate now, desperate to be out.

As I felt the voices behind me, I knew it was our own fault. Joe was missing in the haunted darkness, the evil darkness we had been warned about.

Joe Hardwick (12)

Into The Silence

Howling in the darkness, a wolf, a dog or something unknown. I slowly inched through the forest, twigs snapping.

My mother had said, 'Be careful out there with all those missing people!' But I never listen. Now I know why all those people went missing.

A dead end … I couldn't get out of here, never, it was impossible. I was too tired. I sighed in despair. I fell to the floor sobbing, 'Why did you leave me like this?'

A pale but bloody, ghostly figure appeared in the distance. It started to move towards me as if it was investigating me before coming too close. I slowly clambered up, as if I was going to run away. I tried to back away but there were too many trees. As it slowly moved towards me I could pick out a few details I thought I'd seen before. Black hair covering one eye, thick, black eyeliner.

'Alex?' The figure stared at me as if it was trying to look into my soul, but he was trying to say yes.

But before I could say anything, he was next to me, the last person I had ever seen before I felt a sharp pain. I fell to the ground, clutching my bleeding stomach with my bloody hand. Darkness. Silence

'Raven? Raven? Answer me … please?' said a sobbing voice. 'Raven!' Another voice, 'Raven … if … ' her words drowned into silence.

I had let go forever. I would never see sunlight again.

Destiny Butler-Cook (12)

The Pram

Grace was lying still as a stone, anticipating when it would begin. The lights began to flicker as the clock hands quivered closer to north and south, as dusk spread. The squeaking of the rubber tyres started as they came in contact with the hospital floor, the ruffled black Victorian hood vibrated threateningly as the pram rattled and shook on its nightly search for its passenger. Grace, although in a coma and possibly a dream, could sense the darkness that awaited the innocent baby the pram was looking for. Grace was sure it was a dream as in reality it couldn't be true. Even if this was a dream the pram still made its way to the maternity unit to find a newborn, trundling down the steps, stopping abruptly!

The next morning Grace was sure she could hear soft sobs, but she was in a coma and probably mistaken. While Grace lay on her bed, the nurse tended to her. She had an itch on her nose causing her to scratch. For some reason the nurse seemed surprised, when it suddenly hit Grace that she had moved and was stirring from her long coma. People from all directions crowded round her cubicle to see her awaken.

Things started to settle down and Grace was left on her own. Suddenly, *squeak, squeak, rattle, rattle.* The pram crept closer to her, she let out a piercing scream.

Bbeeeepp! went her monitor as a flatline crossed the screen.

Gabbie Hubbard (12)

The Fire

It was getting dark by the time she started wandering home and as she walked she thought about how quiet it was, just like the story her friend had told her. She stopped and looked behind her nervously, searching the darkness.

'Don't be silly,' she told herself. Just then she heard shouting and saw a vast amount of smoke coming from the next street over. She ran.

Gold and orange flames encased the house before her. There were screams from inside but what could she do? Suddenly, she noticed a man standing on the pavement.

'Help me!' she called. The man shook his head.

'There are people in there!' The man shook his head again.

'Why?' she enquired. Stretching out his hand, the man attempted to grasp her but she leapt backwards.

'Who are you?'

The man took a step towards her, she took a step backwards.

'Can you speak?' she asked. Quite abruptly the man lunged at her, his hand went straight through her middle. An ice-cold chill rushed over her insides. She stumbled backward as he withdrew his hand. It was then that she noticed that even though the wind was blowing not a hair on his head moved.

'Why won't you help me?' she croaked, her mouth dry with fear.

'This is my house,' said the man.

'You live here?'

'No, I die here.'

Florence Nicholson-Lailey (10)

The Haunted Tree House

Many years ago, a man named Cornelius Fletcher bought number 13 Burswood Avenue. He invited some friends round for a house-warming party; but when he told them the address, none of them would come.

'That house is haunted!' they cried. 'We are not going to a party there! A woman was murdered in that very tree house, stabbed in the back, and it's said that her spirit still haunts the inhabitants.'

'What nonsense!' said Cornelius. 'I will sleep in there tonight to prove that you are wrong.'

The next morning, his friends climbed cautiously up the rickety rope ladder to the tree house. They peered round the corner and Cornelius was lying on the floor with a knife in his back. They fled, screaming like lunatics, and no one ever lived in number 13 Burswood Avenue again.

Charlotte Ash (10)

Halloween Horror!

There was once a little girl who ran around our estate all the time wearing masks and ghost costumes. Even at Christmas she would run around with them on. Her granny was a mysterious woman, she always seemed to be about at night and she had a broom that I used to see her cleaning with all the time. Another strange thing I noticed about her was that she didn't let anyone come around to trick or treat at her house. If the postman came round with post you would never see him leave again! Strange isn't it? She had a black cat that she took everywhere with her. It always took big steps and was always wandering around, maybe for mice.

About a year before when her husband died, she told everyone that he died because he was an alcoholic, but I don't think that was how he died. I think it was her who killed him with her broom. I know I have a great imagination, but he was a nice man and I did see him drinking when he was around at ours. A mystery to solve.

At night you could hear funny noises like *booommm* and *hahahaha*. Some nights there were also old women that came round to her house around 12 o'clock, but maybe this was all in my head. Now that I come to think of it, they all looked like her.

I remember hearing *thump! Thump! Thump!* and thinking, *what was that?* I saw four women with broomsticks; they were holding all different kinds of things. I didn't know what they were, but they were walking towards the graveyard. I was going to run into my mum and dad's room to tell them what I had just seen but they wouldn't have believed me. I was still looking out my bedroom window to see what was happening. Suddenly I saw them, there they were, down there and it looked like they were talking to the graves. I went downstairs thinking, *should I look?*

I opened the door slowly, scared to go out. I could hear the women were all laughing and they were playing with dead bodies. I was really terrified now; every hair on my arms was standing on end. They must have seen me because they stopped and said, 'Hello, what are you doing out at this late hour?'

Mrs Patterson said, 'You are the little girl from the house next door.'

I said, 'Yes.' They were all playing with my hair. At that Mrs Patterson lifted me and spun me round. I was really scared. I went to her house and sat on a chair. One of the other women came over to me and asked me did I want a drink of water.

I said, 'Yes please.' She gave me a glass, so I drank it.

'Argh!' That's the last thing I remember until now when things started coming back to me. I recall only when they threw me down on the ground and then I drank the water.

This is a Halloween mystery.

Cora Diamond (11)

Charlotte Trapped For Eternity

The rapidly increasing heat left Charlotte sweltering in her fight for survival. She had been in the dark fuming cave for nearly three hours now. It seemed like something was tapping her on the shoulder but every time she suspiciously glanced back behind her, nothing was there! She stopped dead at the sound of laughter as an unexpected spine-chilling breeze swiftly whipped under her feet.

As 9pm suddenly dawned upon this unforgettable, horrifying night the old damp gravel floor trembled and what seemed like a chandelier smashed into fine glass pieces making a disturbing chiming noise.

Charlotte's bare feet were sliced to shreds from the glass. She made a quick dash to the door but someone, something, somewhere locked her in. Charlotte screamed enough to make grown men tremble 200 miles away but no one could hear her cry!

From that point on she knew she was trapped for eternity.

Sharnise Craig (11)

One-Way Tunnel

I fly homewards, past the shops, down my road, swinging the gate open. I rush across the lawn and the door creaks open. I peer in to be greeted by ominous darkness. I step in calling to Mum. Silence replies.

I creep into the living room and search for the switch. Instead I gently tug a chain and the room alights with candles flicking on everywhere, the fireplace instantaneously lights up, air erupting into swirls of golden flame. It diverts my eye to a leather book beside it. Shaken, I sit beside the warming golden tongues licking the chimney and read. The tale tells of a poor family entrapped by darkness in a tunnel, surviving off water from a fountain and mice scavenged by the cat. They are separated from Miriam the daughter, who so far continues with relative normality.

As I reach this detail a woman thunders in. She has hair navy as night, eyes red like rubies and a black dress which caresses the floor. A biting ghostly wind follows her entrance, making me jump up in horror, falling backwards into ravenous flames.

I am teleported, somersaulting into a dark, airtight space. I hear a hiss, the squeal of a terrified mouse and suddenly Mars, the cat, launches himself into my arms purring.

Charlotte Groves (16)

A Babysitter's Nightmare

Alana had a passion for looking after children and she had babysat children for years but that was in her family, never someone else's. She'd always babysat them in her own house where she felt comfortable.

She sat up for hours one night thinking about putting up posters about herself and she had never thought of it before, so the next morning she got up and printed out posters with her information and her contact details. Fortunately for Alana, she didn't have to wait long before someone contacted her.

The next night she got to babysit someone else's children while the parents went out. The children were no problem putting to bed and so she decided to settle down and watch a DVD. She couldn't find the DVD player so she phoned up the parents and they allowed her to watch the DVD in their bedroom. She went up and got set up and asked the parents if before she settled down could she move the scary clown statue out of the room. But they said that they didn't own a scary clown statue!

Alana tried to speak but couldn't get the words out. She dropped the phone and screamed as the clown moved towards her. The door slammed shut, she was trapped!

After that Alana and the children she was babysitting were never found so if you ever have to babysit, make sure there are no clowns in the house.

Amy Kirkland (12)

Can You Feel It?

Is it me or can any of you feel that shiver? That deep chill that crawls down your back when you're alone, or when the lights are out? That twinge. Those unseen shadowed claws that crumple the cord and throw your mind off balance. Thoughts that you don't want to be thinking, crawl into your mind, keeping you restless.

Alone. Dark.

The sudden shock that keeps you from dozing keeps you awake. Alert. Just in case. Can you feel it now?

Who knows what goes on behind you, when you sit in front of the TV screen. What's crawling up your back? Who's waiting behind the door? What's waiting behind that door? It could be nothing, isn't it always? The corner of your eye catches that glimpse of the unknown.

Quick. Dark.

Did you see it? It's got to be your imagination … right?

Fears leap into your mind, tearing at that already huge hole that's eating away at your stomach. Do you really want to turn around? Do you really want to turn the light back on or are you better off not knowing because what if you turn around or turn on the light? It could be nothing or it could be something else. Something that tears your spine from your mind and whispers nightmares in your ear.

Can you feel it now?

Hannah Chandler (16)

Knock Knock ... Who's There?

Knock knock. What's that? you wonder as you're turning the light off as you are making your way up the dark, creaking stairs. You stop. Turn and think. Is it raining? You uneasily make your way down to the purple curtains at the foot of the stairs and you draw back the curtain slightly. All you can hear is the *pitter-patter* of the rain falling vigorously from the sky above.

From the corner of your eye you see a shadow, you quickly bolt the door and slam the curtains too. You take steps back, slowly. As you climb the stairs that feel more like mountains, you begin to rust, your mind slowly weeps as your fear overtakes. A small mocking sound of your plastered fear creeps into your mind. The phone suddenly pulls you from your thoughts. Ring ... remember. You'd unplugged the phone earlier. How is that possible? *Ring ring.*

Then unexpectedly, a cold, ghost-like shiver slowly makes its way up your spine, gently until you gasp ... and look behind you. You run. Too fast, your legs say. Too slow, your mind says.

Catch your breath, breathe deeply as you gain the courage to slowly walk back down and unbolt the door. Is this the right thing to do? Bolt on again. Flick the light. You grab the nearest thing, a broom. You unbolt the door again and turn the key. Push the handle. *Flick.* The door opens. You stare into the shadow's eyes. It looks back.

Amy Chandler (11)

A Ghostly Tale

I'd always heard rumours about the spooky cottage that stood there before me. People said it was haunted but I wouldn't believe them. I didn't believe in ghosts until the day I investigated the house. So this is how it all began.

As I was walking across the street I heard a hammering noise from that cottage. I thought this was the time to investigate. Going closer to the door, I reached my hand out to the handle. Something strange happened, the door swung open by itself making a loud creaking sound. Slowly, I walked into the room, the door banged shut behind me making my heart beat rapidly with fear.

A strange voice said, 'What are you doing here?'

It was a girl. I could see right through her. My tongue was dry. My words were silent. I tried to get to the door but my legs were frozen. 'I … thought no one lived here. Who are you?'

'It doesn't matter who I am.' A cold shiver went down my spine. 'Just get out of here!'

I ran to the door and slammed it shut behind me. I will find out more, I know I will, I just know it.

Habibah Dukandar (10)

The Boy Who Believed In Ghosts

Once there was a boy called Sam, he lived with his mum, dad, grandma and grandad. Sam went to the cellar and said, 'Ghost!'

Mum ran to the cellar and said, 'What is the matter?'

'There is a ghost. If you do not believe me look down there!'

'There is nothing there,' said Mum.

'But … ' said Sam then they went.

A white flash came. 'Ooo,' came the voice from that white flash. It was the shape of play dough. Sam noticed it was a ghost. 'Do you believe in me?' said the ghost.

'Of course I do,' said Sam.

'Well, if you do tell the others,' said the ghost.

'Okay,' Sam said, so off he went to the living room. 'There is a ghost in the cellar,' said Sam.

'Are you tricking me?' said Mum.

'No!' So Mum went to check.

Ghost!' said Mum.

'Told you!' said Sam.

'Sorry for not believing you,' Mum said. 'Now leave it alone.'

Sannah Shah (11)

The Ghost In The Attic

Once upon a time there was a girl called Emily, who lived in an amazing mansion in the countryside. She was a lovely little girl who lived in the 1800s, and was very kind. Well, that was a very long time ago as we all know and everything was very dull even though her family were one of the richest families around.

One day Emily was sitting in her bedroom playing with her little rag doll, when suddenly she saw a dark shadow move slowly but sneakily across the wall. Emily was not at all worried though because she often saw these shadows and just thought that they were the shadows of her rag dolls, or even herself when they got bigger. But it turned out that these shadows were not what they seemed.

The next night there was a full moon and Emily kept hearing howling, but instead of coming from outside it seemed to be coming from the room on top of her, which was the attic.

Emily stayed up for what seemed like all night listening to the howling but then as the clock chimed 12 there was a last howl and a faint scream, and suddenly the howling stopped. As that happened Emily, who was shivering in fear, pulled her bed cover up and over her head, and never fell asleep that night or for the next 30 nights after that. That was because every night Emily would hear something coming from her attic like howling, the rattling of chains and sometimes even the whispering of her name.

Emily told her parents time after time about what she heard up above her. Eventually her mother and father agreed to sleep in her bedroom with her for one night.

That night her mother put Emily up to bed but when she and Emily's father went up a couple of hours later they stood there with their mouths open wide because all they saw was Emily's bed empty! In poor Emily's bed there was a small note that read: 'Emily has been taken to a better place and if you dare tell anyone about any of this then you will be doomed to a life of Hell, signed the person (or ghost) who wrote this letter.'

After that her mother and father broke down in tears and sadly died but if you walk past this very house in the countryside then you can still hear the screams of poor Emily, the rattling of the ghost's chains and the weeping of her parents as they cry in horror at the note that still lies on Emily's bed.

Shannon Bevan (9)

The Imposter

One chilling Halloween night, Susie was getting ready for a Halloween party she was throwing for pupils that went to her school. She put on her witch hat and looked in her bedroom mirror.

'Wow, I look dazzling in this,' she mumbled to herself whilst looking at her reflection. She had a black gown on which reached down to her feet, along with black sparkling heels that made her look really tall.

She went downstairs where the guests were wearing silly costumes and talking to each other. She really loved guests because she was the type of girl that wanted attention. She then headed towards the kitchen where a dull looking boy called Jack was standing.

'Hey Jack!'

Jack didn't reply back which made Susie think of how him and her were so close, but now that was gone because Susie changed. She looked away to talk to her friends.

As she was reaching for a drink she noticed that everything went silent all of a sudden. She turned around, all the guests had disappeared. Only Jack was standing in her path. She was very confused. She looked more closely at the dull man and noticed he wasn't the Jack she knew; he was an imposter, a fake.

The lights went out. 'Oh my God!'

She screamed loud enough for someone to hear her but no one replied. She could see a little bit of light but after a while she felt a painful sting and something like liquid. Then the world went dark, still and quiet.

Hirra Mahmood (15)

Chiming Bells

Two best friends who were together for most of their lives never really spoke about the afterlife until one day in the park.

'Hey Grace, do you think the afterlife exists?' said Wendy, gazing at the orange sky.

Grace shrugged. 'I don't know … maybe, why do you ask?'

'Because if we die, do you think we can still be best friends?'

'Of course!' smiled Grace.

'But how are we supposed to know that the afterlife exists?'

'I know, why don't we give each other a sign?'

'How? I don't like ghosts!'

'Then how about using bells? Bells make a pleasant noise.'

'Yeah! Okay then, bells it is!'

And so Grace and Wendy made a half-hearted promise.

Three weeks later Grace was caught in a traffic collision and died the following day.

At the day of Grace's funeral, Wendy prayed for Grace's peace. While she was praying, she heard a soft sound of bells.

Wendy looked up and smiled weakly, 'That must be Grace letting me know that the afterlife exists, she's kept her promise.'

Suddenly, the sound of bells got louder and eventually all the visitors turned, starting to panic. The bells jangled and made a terrifying sound as if Grace was in need of help and was going through pain. Wendy covered her ears in fright and shouted for Grace to stop but the sound just kept getting louder. After Wendy screamed her lungs out, the bells finally stopped.

One of the visitors finally said, 'I wonder what the afterlife is like?'

Daphne Siapno (13)

Untitled

My chest feels heavy and sore as I struggle to breathe while desperately yelling and screaming. The cold has crept through my entire body, freezing every muscle and every tiny cell. (They've done a good job this time! I'm so scared I'm practically wetting myself. No seriously.) The room is dark and intimidating, but if you look closer, into the vast darkness and use that thing that people call your brain, this room is not all that it seems. Candles light the empty, derelict corridors that channel around this one main room.

'Whoo …'

Whoops! I've been so caught up in my thoughts I've forgotten my cue! Oh well, now or never. 'I know you're there … please come out.' My voice dies into a whisper. But I mean, come on, could I say anything lamer? Right on cue a white robed figure ambles into the light.

'Ha! I knew you were in there somewhere!' I yell, my voice shaking.

'Whoo!' is all it responds with. The robed figure suddenly dives on my astounded body, punching and thrashing madly at me for all it is worth. Hang on a minute, I don't remember this bit. I am too dumbfounded to fight back; all I manage to do is squeak, 'Help!'

'Cut! Turn the stupid camera off, get that ghost off her,' yells someone I know is trying to help, but all I can think is, *this is one heck of a horror film!*

Megan Elliot (12)

The Letter

Dear Kat,

I can't live like this anymore. We thought we would fit seamlessly back into our old lives, be able to pretend that all was well, that we had not seen Death, that we had not escaped his mangled grasp. But it is not so. Terrifying images reach me in my dreams, Kat, when I am not conscious to control them. I awake screaming, tangled in my too soft sheets, unable to adjust my mind to the calmness of my bedroom. The vivid dreams burn imprints so deeply into the depths of my brain that I cannot be rid of them.

I don't know who I am anymore. My room, filled with my childhood clutter, is no longer recognisable. Books I used to pore over for hours no longer hold meaning. Clothes that used to hug me tightly now hang off my shattered body, for I cannot eat. He took all that I was, Kat, and reduced me to nothing.

Death hides in every shadow. Out there, in the daylight, we don't let ourselves think of these things but here, in the quiet, they creep up, wind their way into your brain like poisonous ivy. He is here Kat, watching me, waiting for the moment when he can snatch me again. I can feel his breath on my neck, hear his laboured panting, waiting, waiting for the perfect moment to strike. Death has all the time in the world.

Heed this warning, Kat; I'll see you on the other side.
Peter.

Emma Jones (14)

Zombie Mayhem

One day in a spooky mansion lived a zombie of a man 200 hundred years old! He was a terrifying 1000 feet tall and was stronger than King Kong. In the mansion there were cobwebs, bats, ghosts and a freaky guest book signed by Frankenstein, Dracula and others. The ghosts made frightful noises like *whoo* and *muhahahaargh*! In the garden lived tens of hundreds of werewolves who were screaming, *hhoowwll*!

There was a brave band of boys called 'The Ghost Slayers'. The three boys' names were Arvin, Elliot and Tom. There was a great battle. There were roars and shrieks.

Finally the boys won. The ghosts never haunted human minds ever again!

Tom Barnes (7)

Ghostly Goings-On!

Once upon a time I saw a ghost. It was white and it was really scary. It was 200 feet tall but only 6 centimetres thick. I went with my friends Amber and Nilay to find the ghost. Amber was terrified! The ghost had disappeared.

At last we found it. We asked the ghost what his name was.

He said, 'Cuddles, I'm a friendly ghost and I live in an old mansion.'

Nilay asked if we could go to Cuddles' house.

Cuddles agreed.

When we got to the mansion Cuddles rang the doorbell. Three ghosts opened the door. We all sat down and had tea, cake and biscuits. When the ghosts ate we could see the food going through them and onto the floor. We all laughed! After, we had to clear the mess up.

Later we unfortunately had to go home. It had been a great time with the ghosts. We all said goodbye and then we went home.

The very next day we came back and had even more fun, we became best friends!

Julia Barnes (7)

Ghost Story

Boys and girls, it all started on the 30th October 2005, in a narrow alleyway where two children who were identical twins lived with their parents. Their names were called Storm and Strawflower. Their parents owned a fish and chip shop therefore Storm and Strawflower ate piles of junk food because they looked after themselves. So you can imagine what they looked like.

The alleyway was very damp and dull with bungalows which had very dark and spooky colours. The one that stood out the most was the one opposite the twins' bungalow. It stood out because it had a broken door, cracks in the windows and it had scruffy curtains like it had been there for centuries.

The children had wanted to go inside that bungalow ever since they could remember. One thundery night the twins thought of a way to get inside the bungalow, there had always been an old man standing at the door of the bungalow. He always told everyone that your body would be devoured if you entered.

On Halloween the twins decided that today was a good day to start their plan. Later that evening the old man went to celebrate Halloween, leaving the house unguarded. The chubby twins tiptoed very nervously across the alleyway. They ran in the bungalow, floorboards were cracking, doors were slamming. Thunder and lightning flashed as the old man was approaching, the children screamed and the old man ran screaming, 'Ghost!'

The twins were never seen again.

Jahmal Taylor (10)

A Ghost In The Wardrobe

On a dark and stormy night Ben was scurrying along the damp streets, heading home after watching a horror movie at the local cinema. Ben walked up the pathway leading to his house.

As Ben closed the front door behind him, the hallway floor creaked beneath his feet as he gradually headed upstairs to his bedroom. He sat down on his bed and put on his pyjamas and began to read a comic. A noise seemed to come from inside his wardrobe. Ben anxiously walked over to his wardrobe and opened it. Nothing was there except for his clothes, shoes and mobile phone. *That's odd,* Ben thought, closing both wardrobe doors slowly.

Minutes later Ben climbed into bed, closed his eyes and pulled the duvet over his head, still shaken about the noise he heard earlier. He tossed to the side and suddenly from the corner of his eye he spotted the wardrobe mysteriously opening … out came a body as white as clouds and a murky grey hole for a face, was it a ghost? It flew swiftly across the moonlit room, closer and closer. Ben trembled as he rapidly sheltered himself with his duvet … He felt it being carefully pulled back, Ben was cold and petrified!

'Ben,' he heard a voice calling. 'Come with me.' The sound of footsteps approached Ben's door.

'Are your lights out Ben?' yelled Mum. Ben got up, the wardrobe doors were closing.

Had the ghost gone forever?

Annie Charalambous (10)

The Chamber Of Death

They hesitantly walked up the rickety stairs that led to the Chamber of Death which waited silently for them, patiently. They could hear whispers that concealed all. Out of the nothingness of the gases present in the atmosphere, a familiar utterance yet again called to them, 'The light is thy foe in thy presence and the dark is thy friend.'

What this voice meant, none knew. Singly the aura of the voice delivered trembles to their limbs from the secret aliveness of the chamber above. As they left their bodies towards unknown reality, they became closer to the inner truth. The last step was most painful, no going back but forward.

Trapped in this dark deserted place for 500 years now, this was their final staircase and there above them was their final abode, the voice muttered once more - a staggering 7,000,000th time, 'The light is thy foe in thy presence and the dark is thy friend.' The enticing awful smell of the damp floor drifted into their noses causing hair to rot instantly.

Finally, the door was a hand's length away. This could change their future like they'd been promised. The leader clutched the cold metal handle and twisted it to reveal … light! The light which they had stayed clear from for 500 years, they fell into the room - dead. 'The light had captured its prey. No sound … just a whisper, 'The light is thy foe in thy presence and the day is thy friend.'

Thaiba Hussain (15)

Poltergeist

Business trip. Lonely hotel room on an ominous deserted corridor. A bump in the night.

'What was that?' I say in a hoarse voice as I pull my cold sweating body from the sheets. A teasing melodious whistling sound seems to linger in the room, merely a murmur in the silence. I scrabble for the switch of the sidelight and hurriedly glance about the room; nothing of course, nothing! Merely my infantile imagination, my continued belief in the monster under my bed, a relic of my childhood. I flick the light off again with a self-depreciating chuckle.

Thud! There was really no mistaking it this time, hands trembling insanely. I locate the light switch once more. A drawer from the dresser lies broken on the floor. I feel ready to vomit as my ears pick up again the sinister, fluctuating whistle. My eyes are watering. As the television throws itself on the floor I let out a silent, breathless scream, the kind that only comes from the most real and terrifying yet equally absurd fears. I manically glance about the room anticipating the next atrocity, my breathing that of a dying animal, quick and heavy. Then the sheets before me ripple, as though a lazy breeze is winding up my bed. I shake my trembling head, lips pursed in fear, tears in my mad half-closed eyes.

Fight or flight? Nothing to fight, flight. From the bed, through the curtains, escape out the window. Freefalling, smiling.

Tom Rowell (16)

Untitled

Two more seconds and he'd be upon us. We hid behind the bushes as we waited for Edgar to go past. He won't let us rest until we're dead. It's a penance for what we've done. He wants to make sure that every person who was there the night he died is dead themselves. It's hard work but Edgar's relentless.

I replay that night in my head. Edgar - mouth twisted in horror, limbs hanging off at odd angles, eyes burning like the pits of Hell. Us - running away, Edgar catching Sam, tearing at him, tearing him into pieces as we watch. Helpless - once Edgar has you there's nothing you can do, it's one man for himself where Edgar is concerned. Scared - if you think you've been scared before, it's nothing compared to how we felt that night, running for our lives. Guilty - watching others die gruesome deaths when I know whose fault it is, when I know who killed Edgar. Me - watching helplessly. Me - feeling scared. Me - feeling guilty. I'm the one who killed him. I'm the one who should have to pay, but I don't.

Now everyone else is dead and I'm the only one left. I hear him coming up the stairs. My heart thuds. He opens the door. I stand up. He walks towards me. I stand strong in the face of death, he's in front of me. I know what's about to happen. Death. Now I'm free. Now Edgar's free. No more guilt.

Eleanor Oliver (14)

Lost Or Not?

The girl was trembling as she walked down the hall, petrified of turning the corner. When she did the faint noise of crying lurked in the empty house. She ran as fast as she could, finally she was in her room.

She was doing her hair and looking in the mirror. A face appeared, her face as grey as the greyest cloud, crying softly but heavily. The girl, Arrabella, was shocked and huddled under her duvet shaking. Unfortunately the ghost was there too.

Arrabella got up the courage to ask, 'What are you doing here?' The ghost didn't reply, all the ghost did was point at what looked like a small door. Arrabella followed curiously behind the ghost who opened the small door and crawled in, along with Arrabella behind. The door slammed shut. Arrabella felt fear edge up her spine, the ghost grabbed her.

They were now in a different world that nobody knew of with water everywhere. The noise was like a factory of shouts. Now in front of them a crowd stood looking up at a weird stage. The two girls pushed past everyone. One peculiar person looked and stared at them until a pickpocket came by.

Finally they were at the front when Arrabella looked up and saw 'Missing girl - Arrabella'. She was stunned and suddenly whisked off her feet and taken away. What was going to happen? All that was left at home was a picture of her waving goodbye.

Emmeline Bryce (12)

Creepy Bob

I woke up at night feeling incredibly thirsty. I decided I would go downstairs and get a drink of water. I lifted up the bed sheets, hopped out of bed, out the door and down the stairs.

I entered the kitchen, taking care to look as it was dark, and fetched a glass, turned the tap on and took a sip.

Oddly, I then saw an odd light shining on the floor. I slowly turned my head around. It was a strange white translucent being, which had a tail. It had a T-shirt that said *Bob*. So I decided to call him Bob. But then I realised there was no messing around. It was a ghost. I was scared.

I fell back to the worktop in the kitchen and I crept around the worktop slowly. There was no movement from The Ghost aka Bob.

I moved towards the ghost, and he moved slightly closer to me. Bob got scared though when I blinked and he flinched back. It seemed that he was more scared of me than I was of him, or was he?

I turned and walked slowly into the hallway with my back facing The Ghost, with my heart racing and wondering just what to do until suddenly, The Ghost appeared in front of me. It came closer to me. It touched me. It walked through me. I became cold, and it felt like there was a breeze then suddenly, a strange bright light surrounded me.

Will Maule (12)

Ghost Story

Tick-tock, tick-tock. I froze. The silence of the night was sending me a message. It was just me, stood alone. Halfway up the rotten staircase. The stairs creaked. I dropped my apple which I had just fetched from the almost empty fruit basket. I took one step up the stairs. I crouched down and picked up my favourite teddy. I clenched him in my hands, the sort of never-letting-go squeeze. There was something behind me, lurking in the darkness of the night. Waiting until the right moment when you stopped panicking and calmed down. I kept thinking, *where is it? Why is it haunting me? What have I done wrong? When is it going to strike?*

I managed to walk up to my room after 15 haunting minutes. I turned on my flashlight and scanned the room. I was out of the ghostly shadows at last. I pulled back my duvet cover and slowly forced myself back into bed.

I was snuggled up again with my teddy and I had my flashlight on so nothing could haunt me anymore. The flashlight flashed and then suddenly *bang!* A big explosion of light burst out from the flashlight, leaving me in complete darkness again. My body went all tense. I couldn't move. Then the door opened to reveal a dark character. I screamed!

Ross Millen (12)

Kniciza

Claire's breath disappeared into icy mist as it escaped from her lungs. She was freezing and hungry but she wasn't going back, not back there. Not while she knew Kniciza was waiting for her. Kniciza was silent. Kniciza was invisible. Kniciza was so much but it was a foul player. It could protect you eternally - but it cost you your life.

It fed off human emotion. It would hide anywhere, watching and waiting. Yet nothing could hurt you when Kniciza was part of you. You were a speck - hardly existent. But you could not think - could not love. What was the point of having a life that you could not control?

Claire shivered and pushed the thought away. Kniciza would not get her, not tonight. She looked around. Was it safe now? It had been a few hours. That was long enough, wasn't it? Milky, stiff fog swamped her as she thought there were waffles at home - comfort food. All right. She would go. But carefully. She had to remember, Kniciza was not fair.

'No, you have a point there,' said a husky voice in her ear, thoughtful and calm. Claire froze.

'But then again life isn't either,' said the voice, in jealous, evil tones. Claire cried out as Kniciza slipped into her very soul, silent and stern. Her eyes misted over then darkened, all emotion lost.
Kniciza had stolen her mind forever.

Hannah Glover (11)

Untitled

The walls felt as though they were closing in on her. The last memory Kati could remember was a curdling scream of her younger brother being torn to shreds at the hands of an unseen menace. He was stripped of his flesh piece by piece, all the while screaming for her to help him, to stop the unbearable pain. And she, Kati, had done nothing to try and stop it instead; she'd backed into a corner of the study, whimpering for that thing to leave her alone. She was nine years old and she just sat there as a five-year-old boy was becoming frayed like her sleeves.

As the screams became silence, she prayed that the *thing* that had murdered poor innocent Danny, had ripped and ripped until only a fragile skeleton was left, was satisfied enough to leave her be. But of course fate never worked that way. The creature was slowly materialising into a visible form. As the creature shape became fully formed, Kati's whimpering was stunned into silence. She looked into the monster's eyes to see a bottomless pit of hunger, no emotion but greed shone in those ghostly eyes. It was coming towards her but she couldn't bear the thought of what that creature really was …

'Dad?'

Emily Jane Knight (14)

Horror Ivy

The sky was pitch-black and the air was cold. I walked up to the decaying, abandoned house. It was covered in ivy crawling up the walls, hunting for prey as it went.

I thought the old folk tale was false so I stupidly sputtered out that I would prove them wrong.

I walked up to the wall, staring at the gruesome ivy. It was not normal ivy but a fierce black. Well, that's what I suspected anyway. Despite the dreaded beating of my heart raising my chest like waves in the ocean I leant forward and picked one strand of the black, horror ivy. Even my own sister warned me not to for I would become just a pile of mouldy, deserted bones on the floor.

Suddenly the air became a hurricane. My vision became blank. I was going to die! Then, before I could open my mouth to scream, my legs lost balance, they disappeared! I shouted for help ...

But before I knew it I was just a pile of mouldy, deserted bones on the floor.

The village became silent once again.

Molly Cascarina (11)

Safe And Sound

It was silent, her fingertips ghosting over the brittle woodwork before her. A cold sweat had broken out along her forehead, sending shivers down her spine. A warm sensation crept along her arm. She felt it, the rough fingertips caressing her skin.

She hovered by the threshold of the door. The small boxed-in room was silent and bare, the dry walls seemingly closing in around her. The dark timber contrasting with the pale light seeping through the window. With little light, the room was cast into a world of shadows that stretched out like cats, their claws working into the grooves upon the walls. As she finally found the courage to wrap her hand around the handle, a weird feeling came over her. The will to turn it disappeared like the flick of a light switch.

Strange, she thought. Shaking it off as nerves she took hold of the handle. *Turn it! Turn it!* Determination coursed through her body, wondering what lurked on the other side. Then she felt it, a cold breeze, even though no window was open. Something grasped her wrist. Another clutched her around the stomach. Rough fingers caressed her skin, cascading down to the hollow of her elbow where they gripped, applying pressure. The arm across her middle tugged gently, urging her away from the door.

Momentarily, she let it tug her back but then the sheer will and determination returned. Wrenching herself away, she lunged forwards.

A whisper heard in the air, 'No!'

She turned it.

Holly Elliott (14)

A Deadly Lullaby

The only strange thing he'd noticed when he looked out of the window on that autumnal night was the agitated manner of the wind. It howled and smashed against the trees, twisting their branches into gruesome contortions. He shivered and closed the curtains, shutting out the darkness. His candle flickered on his writing desk and a moth tapped against the window, like a tiny heartbeat.

The house was as silent and still as if it were deep under the ocean. His bedchamber was the only room with a glow of light. He was alone in the house. Alice had gone to stay with her sick mother and the cook, Jefferson, had left to visit his brother in London. He lay on his bed, feeling somewhat comforted by the silence, yet slightly unnerved. He blew the candle flame out with one sharp breath.

He awoke in the later hours of that dark, dark night to the sound of children whispering. His body froze. The wind had stopped. The whispering became louder and the children sounded frightened. There were hundreds of voices, although he could not make out what they were saying. *I must be dreaming,* he realised, *this is a nightmare.* He closed his eyes tight and wished himself awake. The air turned cold and the sound of desperate screams filled the house. White, translucent heads with black eyes and tiny mouths glided into his room. They were whispering and hissing. He opened his eyes. He screamed, but his voice was a whisper. The room had filled with heads, each one empty and searching. The whispering was feverish and violent, only now could he hear the words.

Alice and Jefferson returned in the early hours on Sunday morning. When they entered the master's bedchamber, they were greeted with a haunted whisper from a severed head which was pinned to the wall.

Charlie Willis (16)

Anna

Anna woke up to a gunshot, a gunshot that had made her jump out of bed before she was fully awake. The second gunshot had her running down the stairs and all she heard was the front door slam shut. She ran down the last few stairs and into the living room in search of her mother. As she turned the corner she could see a silhouette of her mother in the twilight. Her mother got up and walked past Anna and into the hallway. She followed her mother until her mother began to walk slowly up the stairs.

A minute later her mother walked back down the stairs as slowly as before and picked up the phone.

'My daughter's dead,' Anna's mother said softly to the person on the other end of the phone.

Anna blinked and looked at her mother as if she were mad, she had to be mad. Anna was standing there very much alive.

'What are you talking about Mum?' Anna said, hysteria creeping into her voice.

She tried to touch her mother but her hand seemed to just go through her. She backed away, screaming at the top of her voice for help as she ran up the stairs away from her mother. She stopped in front of the door to her room and looked inside and saw the answer to her confusion and terror … Anna's body lay on the bed, a gunshot wound to her head.

Ellie Ackroyd (12)

Revenge Of Black Mist

It was one dark, stormy night when Jack and Amy were in their new white Audi. They were returning from their robbery mission to capture the rare Black Mist diamond. This diamond was not ordinary. It was one of a kind which had a rare beast trapped inside called Black Mist. The Black Mist was perfectly fine until Jack had to say the words, 'Release, be released to the darkness,' to set Black Mist free. They were so happy that their mission was complete.

The next day they woke up bright and early to find out their new mission was to go to the Sauria Forest to accomplish the task of bringing a mummy back to life. During their mission, they had to take the route of passing a short lightened tunnel.

On their way to the forest, they arrived at the tunnel. At first they went at a slow speed.

After five minutes driving, they wondered how long it was and when it would end. So they started driving faster. Suddenly, with the blink of an eye, the lights started flashing and eventually turned off. They were petrified and drove faster and faster until their car stopped and spun around on its own. They were confused, they had no more control of their car and couldn't get out. They were trapped!

They had no idea what was happening. Then Black Mist appeared outside of the car with thousands of veins in an eye, he drew everyone's attention. He put his huge purple hand on top of the car and pushed as hard as he could. This made Jack and Amy so scared they were shivering. But Black Mist didn't care. He wanted his revenge and put death fumes of his poisonous gas into the car. They suffocated so hard that they died and their eyeballs fell out. Black Mist was overjoyed, he took their eyeballs and crushed them with his humongous feet.

Bryan Neermul (10)

After You Read This, It Is Going To Self-Destruct

Emily and Layla are best friends and they have sleepovers every Friday and they are going to again but unfortunately it might not turn out so well.

The day of the sleepover they went out without their parents. Their parents never came back but they were so tired that they forgot and fell asleep on the swings, unaware of what was going to happen next.

The next day an evil doctor gave them medicine to make them insane so he could cure them and be rich. He did cure them and he was on the stage for the Nobel Prize and a cure came out.

The girls ingeniously figured out what was going on and bam! The doctor was sued and the next day he was dead. The two girls were in the money. The blood dripped on the money and the laughs came again.

Do you know how I know this? Because I am the doctor!

Self-destruction will commence in five seconds …

Melisa Kaplanbasoglu (11)

The Scary Clown From A UFO - An Extract

Out in the spine-chilling, dark, misty garden something was rattling amongst the twined, twisted thorny rose bushes, but they couldn't figure out what it was.

At this time the family, including Bobby, came out into the garden, there seemed to be nothing there. Suddenly they spotted a figure approaching them. Bobby's parents quickly took the children and ran in the house, locking the door behind them. Everyone grabbed an object to defend themselves. The family froze with fright. They paused a second or two to hear … and suddenly heard a loud knock at the front door.

Whoever was at the door crept up to look through the dirty, crooked, dusty window and started to laugh out loud saying, 'Let me in!' Bobby thought it was a clown at first but his mum and dad disagreed.

After that Bobby went to his bedroom in a sulky mood because his parents disagreed with him. Looking out from his bedroom window he undoubtedly saw flashing lights shaping to be a UFO.

At that moment he thought the aliens had landed. He sneakily opened his school bag and chucked in the following objects: a baseball bat in case he needed it for self-defence, his big fishing net to catch whatever was to there and a fishing rod to hook them from high up in the trees.

While making a ghastly plan Bobby heard noises calling to him constantly. It sounded like a ghostly vampire …

Adem Hilmi (10)

The Corpse

Laura rolled her eyes. 'Fine, I'll go in if it shuts you all up!' She walked up three creaky stairs that led to the abandoned house. There was no such thing as ghosts or monsters so there was nothing to be afraid of. Laura pushed the door open and it creaked.

'So cheesy,' she muttered to herself. Something dropped from the ceiling; Laura ducked and looked up. *Just a bird,* she told herself. Laura thought about standing around for a while then walking out casually to her friends, she shook her head, she needed to prove to herself that she was brave.

She took a step up the stairs but it caved in. She walked into what used to be a living room and there it was, a dead man's body was sitting in the armchair. Laura stopped, its eyes locked with hers, she shrieked and ran into the kitchen. Laura skidded on the floor and felt something grab her ankle. Laura looked up off the floor, blood was splattered all over the kitchen. She jumped up and ran out the door, leaving it open.

Laura ran back to her friends, they laughed at her but she screamed, 'Run!' and then broke out into a sprint and ran home.

After a restless night's sleep, Laura got out of bed and turned on the TV to the news. Three teenagers were reported dead. Laura's face drained of blood and her stomach went tight.

Andrea Caroline Pratt (14)

The Silly Ghost

In the land, what can you see? Can you see a sun shining bright, the moon or a butterfly? It's not any of those. I will tell you a story that nobody knows because it happened years ago. I hope that you won't be too scared.

In a little village a ghost appeared and said, 'Who comes my way and touches my nose will certainly die!'

One day an old man was poisoned because he banged into the silly old ghost's nose. The old man didn't die; he just fell asleep with spots on his face!

The ghost cried, 'Whoopee, whoopee, a person died!' But actually it was only a silly thought. Even so she went on saying, 'Whoopee! Whoopee!' all day long until she got sleepy doing that and went to bed.

Suddenly, *bang, bang, bang!* The museum clock rang so hard that the ghost woke up. She went out and saw a man cutting wood. The ghost wanted to see better what the man was doing so she leaned so much that the man cut her nose without even knowing it.

The ghost was cross. She realised that she couldn't make people die or even fall asleep! She picked her nose from the ground and tried to stick it back on with Sellotape. The result wasn't that great so the ghost was so ashamed that she vanished and was never seen again.

Maya Sofia Crasmaru (6)

Train To Hell

Fifty years ago, in the middle of town, there stood a fair. People loved this fair and families went often until a member of one died on one of the roller coasters. This person was dressed as a clown and his lap bar came loose and he fell out and then died. There is a myth that the man weirdly became a clown ghost and haunts the site where he died.

Fifty years after that, a ghost train was built over the place where he died on the fair. Everyone who goes in has witnessed the reality of the ghost clown and some have witnessed the capability of it. Some people have gone in before and never come out!

Me and my mate were walking into town when a boy over the road dared us to go into the ghost train. We were buying our tickets; the man who served us looked like he should be inside. We sat down in the carriage and the bar came down and locked very tightly. We entered with ghostly noises, a bit obvious seeing as it was a ghost train. Lights flashing, ghosts jumping out, every once in a while we saw human movements. I had an idea what it was, it was the clown.

The lights went off then back on again. My mate was gone, I heard this evil giggle. I knew it was going to be me next. I carried on this nightmare that was slowly becoming reality. The lights went off again then came back on. A snarling realistic clown faced me …

Abbi Davies (12)

The Muddy Hand!

Jack and Mark were watching 'The Muddy Hand 2', they were scared. The muddy hand grabs its prey around the neck and squeezes until the eyeballs pop out of their sockets, turning them into demons. The hand had just turned the last victim into a demon, who will go prowling the streets at night when everyone is asleep.

When the film had finished they went to bed. Jack said he wouldn't go to sleep because he was scared but Mark said it wasn't real, and to go to sleep.

Later that night Jack woke up and disturbed Mark. They heard a noise downstairs, it sounded like tapping. Jack said it might be the hand but Mark said it wasn't. They went downstairs with a cricket bat to protect themselves. They saw muddy patches on the floor in the living room.

Suddenly the tapping seemed to come from behind the sofa, they checked it out when something jumped from behind the sofa and had Mark around his neck but it wasn't the hand or the demon, it was their cat. Then they knew that it was the cat's claws making the tapping noise and the muddy patches weren't mud, they were cookie crumbs.

They went to their bed with nothing to worry about when two hands, which weren't attached to arms, had them around their necks and turned them into demons.

If you see the demons run for your life and beware, they can smell you!

Josh Brookes (12)

The Shadow

She lay there pretending to be asleep, trying as hard as she could but couldn't. Everything was calm but the one thing that was keeping her awake was the silhouetted shadow at the other end of the room. It was looking directly at her and she knew it was, she dared not open her eyes.

It began moving and that was strange, it was a shadow but you could hear its every move. She tried to reach for the light switch, but there was some kind of force holding her hand away. She had to do something but what? She could only whimper in fear and hope for the shadow to disappear.

The shadow was creeping nearer. She could feel it. It was now leaning over her. Her heart was pounding in her chest, like someone beating on a very tight African drum at a very unsteady rhythm. She could feel it breathe.

She wanted to go wake her mum and make it disappear. The heavy breathing was rushing amongst her hair and quivering face. She shook with fear. It was one or the other, stay there and wonder what's going to happen next or go downstairs. She took a deep breath, pulled back the quilt and …

Jessica Groom (10)

Haunted House

One dark gloomy day, Sam, Georgar and Toby decided to play hide-and-seek. They asked their big sister Kelly to play with them. Kelly was counting and Sam, Georgar and Toby were hiding. Toby asked if they could hide in the cupboard. Sam and Georgar agreed so they went and hid in the dark brown cupboard. They did not realise that this was a magic cupboard.

This magic cupboard flew, leaving a puff of smoke behind into the dark blue sky as Sam, Georgar and Toby were feeling shaken.

At last it landed on a rough surface. Sam, Georgar and Toby opened the cupboard. It was a rather strange place. In front of this place it had a mysterious house. Sam, Georgar and Toby opened the door and went inside the haunted house. It was dark and creepy, there were cobwebs everywhere. It was old and rusty because no one had lived in it for a long time but then they got locked in!

Then Toby found a note saying: 'To get out you must find the key until midnight approaches.'

'Quick,' whispered Toby. 'Let's find the key.' The team set off to find the key; they kept on looking at the same place.

A while later they looked at different places.

'Oh no,' warned Sam. 'Five minutes to midnight, let's get a move on.'

They searched everywhere, at last Georgar found the key. They all ran to the door. They quickly unlocked the door and ran into the cupboard. With a puff of smoke it flew back to where it was. Sam, Georgar and Toby quickly got out.

Kelly found them and laughed. 'Were you hot in there?'

After that day they never went into the cupboard ever again.

Karvya Kaneswaran (8)

Welcome To My World

Her cool hand soothes my brow, it brushes my burning cheek. She holds my drooping head, offers a cooling liquid to my parched lips. Frowning deeply, a furrowed brow, her sombre gaze lifts to my father, he motions with a mournful movement of his head. His mouth is tight, a straight line across his handsome face.

My sobbing mother sits on my crumpled bed. Close. She grips my hand, my weak limp hand. Her broken voice, 'Don't leave us now. No, not now.'

My heavy eyes close …drifting into dreamless sleep.

She's standing there, again, staring out of the rain-speckled window.

Sparkling white jewels meander aimlessly down the pane. She turns to meet my gaze. Her shabby dress, grubby and grey, draped shapelessly around her tiny frame; clutching her tattered rag doll she strikes a pathetic pose. A dirty face, stained with the tracks of millions of tears, haunts me. Hopelessness. Yet through this despair her sapphire eyes shine now with promises of hope and love. Smiling her shy welcome, glad I am awake; she lifts her delicate hand in greeting. Barefoot, she silently moves to my bed. I take her proffered hand in mine. Timid, friendly smiles pass between us, warming my whole being. She leans closer … an icy whisper of breath envelops my soul.

Words echo in my mind. 'Welcome to my world.' Eyes aglow … eyes of glass … slowed heartbeat … stilled heartbeat … shallow breath … breath 'no more.

She needs a friend. I am her friend.

Ally Laver (18)

It

It was a sunny day when I was walking through the woods. As I got deeper and deeper I realised something was not right. As I looked up to the sky a big black cloud came at me. I heard rattling in the woods so I ran and fell over.

I had landed at the end of a long path with a graveyard outside of a big house. I could hear a little girl whispering my name saying, 'Walk towards the house.'

As I got to the door I went to knock but it opened slowly. I walked in; I was looking in every door. I went to open the door but it was locked. There was a key on the floor. I opened the door and in there was a book. I opened it; it looked out of the window and saw hands coming out from the ground and zombies walking towards me. I ran screaming and they came in through the floorboards. So I ran and went to run out the backdoor but there were zombies so I ran out the front door, round down the path.

The gates were closed and zombies grabbed me and I turned into a zombie. The book shut, the door locked and the key dropped on the floor as I went underground.

So now I lie there and wait for a new person to open the book. We shall chase them so we have a load of people to join us.

Mitch Gleed (12)

Me And The Deadly Ghost

E very night when I go to bed I always seem to hear a knocking sound, as if something or someone is tapping at the window, so every night I go to the window, there's nothing there. I go back to bed and once I'm in bed I hear the tapping sound again. I go back to the window, then all of a sudden there is a little boy standing on the front of my garden.

I run downstairs open the front door and the little boy is not there anymore. I run as fast as I can back up the stairs, I am in my room, in my bed, shaking with the covers over my head then all of a sudden, I hear someone saying, 'I'm coming to get you!'

It sounds like someone is in my room. I look and there is no one there so I shout, 'Show yourself.' There he is with blood coming out of his eyes and cuts all over his body.

I ask him in a terrified voice, 'What do you want from me?'

He says back, in a deep scary voice, 'I want your life!'

Then I faint. I wake up and the next minute you know I have cuts all over my body, I try to get my mum and dad but I can't open the door as my hands are just going straight through the door handle, then I look in the mirror ... I realise I am a ghost!

Leah McMillan (13)
Benfield School, Newcastle Upon Tyne

Re-Awakening

I watch. I wait. I think of my worst fears. Then it appears; I stare Death in the face. I am now looking straight into its eyes, dare I blink? I must not lose eye contact with this weird haunting. This ghost of a lost world. I must blink, my eyes staring, however I still stare.

I sniff up. I can smell the fear. The fear of a terrified boy, suddenly I build the courage to examine the spooky figure. It's like a zombie, it's breathing like it's got asthma.

The tension is building. Three more hours till dawn, can I last that long? My fingers twitching, I need to make the first move. However, I can't do it. This is a life and death situation, can I last? Out of nowhere, it pounces ...

Then I wake up in a church, my father carrying a coffin with my name on it ... I'm at my own funeral!

Joe Lowrey (12)
Benfield School, Newcastle Upon Tyne

Poltergeist

In an average town, in an average place, something very unusual occurs every full moon.

A poltergeist rises from the grave, and haunts the town, searching for a soul to consume. The poltergeist is a former soldier who deserted his squad so he was sent to be hanged. His corpse was cremated and his ashes were scattered in the wind. The poltergeist haunts this place since he was never laid to rest and consumes souls to fill an emptiness in his soul. The poltergeist always leaves a trail of ectoplasm wherever he goes. The poltergeist is relentless and won't stop till he is satisfied.

Normally the town sacrifices a small animal such as a sheep to the poltergeist but this night was different, the town was out of sheep so they had to make a difficult choice of sacrificing one of their own.

One child decided to take the burden and offered to be sacrificed to the creature.

The child's name was Jack; he had been an orphan since birth. During his time at the orphanage he had been treated as a runt. He had trouble succeeding at school, always failing tests and starting fights.

Tonight Jack was standing in the graveyard waiting for the ghost. Around midnight he knew it was coming when a sea of ectoplasm was surging towards him …

Jake Smith
Benfield School, Newcastle Upon Tyne

My Ghost Story

There once was a man called Steve who lived in a big mansion with his wife Mary. Twelve years ago Steve was rich and he kicked his brother out of his house because his brother always used to argue with him. Eventually Steve's brother got sick of him and one night crept through the window and killed Steve.

A few weeks later, after Steve died, his wife Mary moved somewhere else. Steve was 30 when he died and his brother was 24. Since that every day Steve died he would haunt the house he'd lived in.

One day some children were walking around when all of a sudden they saw Steve's house. One boy said, 'I've heard stories about this place, they say it's haunted, do you want to go in?' The boys agreed with him so the boys headed over. Unfortunately the gate had a lock on.

One of the boys said, 'How can we get in there?'

'Let's go find something to hit it with,' replied the other boy.

So they searched the woods until they finally found a block of wood.

'Let's use this,' said the littlest boy. The boys threw the block of wood at the gate many times till it finally came off. They opened the gates then walked through. They slowly walked into the house and were being quiet.

One boy whispered, 'Does anyone live here?'

'No, a man died here 12 years ago,' replied the other boy.

The boys had a look around the house and it was just dusty everywhere and there were pictures of a woman and a man. They slowly walked upstairs and every step they took the stairs would creak. Then, all of a sudden, the boys heard a *bang* coming from upstairs. They ran up and split up. They all checked the bedrooms. One boy saw a big hole in the wall so he climbed through to see what was there. All the boys heard a scream so they ran into that room and couldn't find their friend, also there wasn't a hole anymore. There were four boys left.

One boy said, 'I'm going downstairs.' So he quietly walked downstairs then he heard thumping. He looked behind him and all he could hear was someone laughing and a picture floating so he sprinted down the stairs but just on the last step the floor collapsed and the boy screamed until you couldn't hear him anymore.

There were three boys left and one said, 'I want to go home!' So he ran home screaming.

The other boys stayed. They went into the bathroom and on the mirror there was writing saying: 'Why are you in my house?'

The boys said, 'Please don't kill us; we just wanted to see the house.'

The writing cleared and then said: 'You've got 5 seconds to get out. 5 … 4 … 3 …' Then the boys ran for the door.

Someone shouted, 'Too late!' The doors locked and they saw a ghost behind them. They couldn't believe it. Next moment Steve set the house on fire and laughed and vanished. The two boys died.

Brooke Gibson (13)
Benfield School, Newcastle Upon Tyne

The Secrets Of The Orphanage

It was a dark and stormy night and all the children at the orphanage were fast asleep but little Timmy was still awake.

He couldn't sleep as he was hearing noises, the noises continued. There was tapping at the window and banging from the floorboards as if someone from underground was trying to break free. It got louder. Timmy felt a cold breeze on the back of his neck; he pulled the blanket over his head.

Five minutes later he heard his friend call his name. He looked. Jonny was standing at the end of his bed. Timmy was wondering what Jonny was doing in his room.

Jonny whispered, 'Come with me, come please Timmy,' in a sweet but scary voice. Jonny took Timmy by the wrist and headed to the wall and just walked through.

Timmy tried to get back to bed but he was being pulled by the wrist. Suddenly he was in a strange place, a carnival, he supposed. They walked to the haunted ghost train and the train started even though nobody was there.

Jonny whispered, 'Come with me Timmy, it's not that scary.' When all of a sudden something grabbed Timmy by the neck and pulled him back against the wall. Jonny came and stood in front of him.

'Silly boy Timmy,' he whispered as he morphed into a horrible disgusting beast. Then he walked towards him and sucked Timmy's soul right out his body.

Timmy was never seen again although children in the orphanage continued to complain of ghosts in their rooms.

Rhiannon Bell (13)
Benfield School, Newcastle Upon Tyne

The Visitor

It became clear, I wasn't alone. Fear covered every inch of my body and mind. I was losing it - that was the only explanation, but there was no time to think about that now, for it became clear my company wanted more than a quick hello.

I could feel the ghost-like creature creeping nearer and nearer. Every time it came nearer I had a mini cardiac arrest. My legs trembled as I got off the bed but nothing could prepare me for what happened next.

I saw it - the creature, but it wasn't a creature, for it was a man - a dead man. A dead man that seemed every bit alive! My instinct was to run but there was no way about it and then it hit me. This was how I was going to die, killed by a dead man in the heart of the night.

Susan Newton (14)
Carr Hill High School, Preston

The Calling

It was a cold, dark, unforgiving night and the streets of Seattle were empty and silent. Too silent. A silence so thick it was like a large blanket had been placed over everything. The eerie calmness was deafening. Nobody could help comparing this lifeless, cold, chilling street to the hive of activity it was during the day. The atmosphere was blood-curdling enough to chill anyone's heart and death was in the air. There were discarded newspapers and plastic bags whirling in the atmosphere and the street lights kept quivering on and off, on and off, on and off.

There was a peculiar small child walking down these litter-ridden streets. She'd lost her mum and was now searching for her, calling out her name. Her innocent cries were enough to melt even the coldest of hearts but little did she know she wouldn't be searching for much longer.

It was only as the ghost made his way to the main street did he smell the mouth-watering stench of fresh flesh and the beating of a lonely small child's heart as they walked through the deserted streets. How or why the child was there didn't matter to him. The ghost only had one thought on his mind: blood.

Bethany Ackers (13)
Carr Hill High School, Preston

Ghost Story

'May her gentle soul rest in peace.'

'Amen,' chorused everyone.

'Andy, it's time to go home.'

'Okay Mum.'

'Don't leave me,' whispered a voice.

'Who's there?' asked Andy.

'Andy hurry up.'

'Coming Mum.'

'It's me,' replied the voice. 'Follow the staircase to meet me.'

'Another day please, I'm sorry. I've got to go.' But before I could get into a car a white flash entered the car before me. I entered the car shocked, not sure if I was in a dream or it was real. I looked round the car to look for something unusual but everything was normal from the car into the house, form the house into my room.

'Andy, it's time for dinner,' called Mum.

'Coming.' Leaving the door open I went to change my clothes but first I decided to calm myself down by getting some fresh air. But something white passed through me. Laughter arose from nowhere.

'Who's there?' I asked.

'Use the ladder, follow us!' was all I heard.

The door I left open was now shut. Nowhere to run, nowhere to hide. Just me and the ghost, or was it ghosts? Out of the darkness, a tiny light shone on a book I'd abandoned for years. I was getting closer to the book. The voice was getting louder and louder.

I got the book in my hand and as I opened the book, the verse I saw was meant for me. It said: 'Call on the name of Jesus and all your problems shall be solved.' Then I said, 'All these ghostly ghosts that are scaring me right now, Jesus please take control.'

Nothing happened at first but then I heard voices saying, 'No, have mercy on us, move! We came to the wrong destination!'

Then I asked myself, 'Was that me that spoke?' Then I felt peace soothing my soul. Happily I went down the stairs for dinner. The battle with ghosts was over at last.

Chisom Adaeze Egwuatu (11)
Corona Secondary School, Nigeria

The Deadly Surprise

My heart was pounding as the rain was falling. As I approached a dark street, all the houses were dark and decorated with bats, carved pumpkins, tissue mummies, rubber skeletons. Every house I turned to made me shiver with fear. I didn't understand why I was scared, I just felt bad coming home late to spend Halloween with my family. I was sure Susan wanted to murder me and the girls would be so disappointed that I was not there to take pictures of them in their Halloween costumes and I promised.

With guilt still crowding my heart I took the familiar turn to my house. To my surprise, the whole street was dark and silent and really scary. I smiled to myself thinking that my street would win the best decorated street.

On getting to my house the house was really dark, scary but well decorated. I couldn't hold back my laughter; Susan, my wife, did a splendid job with the house.

I opened the door and to my surprise there were no two little girls running to give their old man a hug. I called out for Susan, no answer. I felt terror take over me. I ran to the kitchen only to find a knife, a blood dripping knife on the table. Thunder struck and I saw … I saw a corpse! A dead body of a little girl lying down in a puddle of blood. Looking at the body I thought I was going to pass out, the girl was my first daughter.

I couldn't react because of the scream I heard upstairs. I ran so fast, I thought I was flying. I slowly opened the door of the girls' room and I saw footprints, bloody footprints. I followed the footprints to my bedroom, the door had bloodstains and the carpet under the door was soaked … soaked with blood. I was terrified.

Words couldn't describe how I felt. I heard a sharp screech and cry of help. With shaking hands I opened the door only to find my baby girl, she was only two, lying dead on the floor and my wife soaked in blood gasping for air. I ran towards her and held her close.

'Who did this?' I asked, terrified of the answer.

'Ha-ha-rry,' she said in pain.

'Who's Harry?' I asked. She didn't reply.

I looked at her as she shut her eyes and didn't move then it hit me, I did this to my family. I was never there for them and when they needed me the most I was in a cramped up office sorting out documents. I just sat down crying my eyes out, my whole family was gone. I couldn't think straight, I just ran down to the kitchen and took a knife, then thunder struck. I felt scared.

I lifted up the knife and struck myself with it, suddenly the lights came on and my wife, my two girls and my neighbours came out dressed in Halloween costumes and screamed, 'Happy Halloween Harry!'

Tomilola Kosoko (12)
Corona Secondary School, Nigeria

What A Prank

R*ring rring!* Lola picks up her phone, it is her brother. 'Jack what is it now?'

'Sis, can you come home right now? Argh! Something is after me! Help, help!'

'Yeah right Jack.' And she cuts the phone. But something is still bugging her. What if it is real? She would never forgive herself.

'Get out of my way!' Lola says in a rush to get home. She gets home and hears an eerie scream. She walks into the house and what does she see? Paint. Is that paint? She goes closer to find out and sees that it is cold blood. She is too stunned to speak which is good because she hears the scream again. This time closer.

She walks up the staircase in the direction of the scream. On her way she sees more blobs of blood. She gets to her brother's room and she sees a box. She opens it and finds her brother chopped up and packaged.

'Argh!' Now she finds her voice and screams. But then she hears a giggle behind her. She checks under the bed and finds her brother and his friends under the bed.

'Gotcha! April fool!'

'Ooo! Wait till I get my hands on them.' But then something grabs her by the shoulder. She turns, it's Jack. She looks down, she sees Jack. Then she says, 'Jack?'

'I'm here sis,' Jack says from under the bed.

'If you are there, then who is this?'

They all look up and hear evil laughter, 'Buah-ha-ha-ha!'

'Oh no! Argh!'

Dumebi Vanessa Okoh (12)
Corona Secondary School, Nigeria

The Lost Children

Once upon a time, there was a myth about the ghost of the castle night. A family died and all that remained was their uncle and children, Drake and Josh who had to live with their uncle in the castle. Their uncle never told them about the ghost of the castle. When their uncle died a mysterious death, the children were forced to live on their own.

One noisy and windy night, the children were so uncomfortable they couldn't sleep. They heard a voice calling them, 'Drake, Josh,' repeatedly. They decided to follow the voice. They reached the library part of the castle and saw a white looking creature floating on air. Before they could turn around the door was locked. Then they heard an evil laugh.

After a day they became hungry. Drake remembered what his uncle used to do - there was a food store inside each room. So he felt the bookshelf and there the food was.

Outside the room people thought the children were lost so they turned the castle into a hotel. People stayed there each night. The children banged the door of the room for anyone to hear them.

There was a married couple with no children staying at the hotel. They always wished to have a child.

One night as usual the knocking continued. When the couple heard it they were afraid at first but later decided to follow the noise. They found out that the noise led them to a door. The door was now very weak and feeble so it could break easily. They brought out Drake and Josh. The children were adopted by the couple.

But that was not all; the ghost kept haunting the house. One night the ghost appeared in physical form. Drake found out the problem so he buried the ghost's coffin to rest in peace. The curse was lifted, the house was back to its normal form and they lived happily ever after.

Etinosa Victor Osaikhuwhomwan (12)
Corona Secondary School, Nigeria

Victor

There once lived a lady called Mrs Wallace, she had one son and one daughter but sadly her husband died.

One stormy night someone knocked on Mrs Wallace's door. Mrs Wallace slowly opened the door and saw an old lady standing outside.

'Hello, I suppose your name is Mrs Wallace.' The strange lady said, calmly.

'Of course,' replied Mrs Wallace. 'You better come in then.'

'You might be wondering who I am, I am maid who is no longer wanted.' The maid said, looking down and with a flash of lightning she was gone.

The next morning after breakfast the music room curtains were drawn and their daughter, Molly, was studying in it. In the bedroom Larry, her son, was studying in it. Mrs Wallace was standing in the dining room.

Suddenly she heard someone crying. She dashed to the bedroom but Larry wasn't crying so she went to Molly's room but she wasn't crying either.

'Who was crying? Mrs Wallace said to Molly.

'It might have been Victor, Mum,' Molly said.

'Who's Victor?' said Mrs Wallace.

'The boy who wanted to play on the piano but I didn't let him. He ran outside five minutes ago,' said Molly.

'But I locked the door!' However the door was unlocked …

Anjum Mamon (10)
Cyril Jackson Primary School, Limehouse

The Mysterious Television

It was a stormy night in London. All was fine until a boy called Jack saw his TV cut out. This wouldn't normally bother him but his parents were away for the weekend, he was alone. Jack whispered to himself, 'I think I will go to bed.'

As Jack got to the top of the stairs he heard a voice. 'Yes I am very sleepy,' it said. Jack thought it was the dog but it was not. He then walked to the TV, it was off. All of a sudden a new voice was heard.

'Cat was that you?' Jack said aloud. Jack ran to the TV and kicked it into the bin; he was beginning to feel afraid in his own home.

Somehow he was able to sleep, the house fell silent.

8.30am, morning - Jack got out of bed to see TVs all over him. Voices were in his head. In the wall, on the floor, they were everywhere. The doorbell rang. Jack ran to the door to see a delivery man with a thousand TVs. Would Jack make it out alive or would it be TV World forever?

Louie Keir (10)
Cyril Jackson Primary School, Limehouse

The Girl Who Screamed For The First Time

One night there was a girl called Violet. She was 11 years old and she lived with her brother, Charlie, and her mum. Her parents had divorced three years ago. Before she went to bed, she checked the house to see if everyone was asleep. Violet never screamed in her life. So then she went off to sleep.

Violet woke up at 1am to have a glass of water because her throat was very dry. She went to the kitchen but suddenly she surprisingly found a big wooden box with lots of blood on it, deadly, horrifying blood. Violet also found a dagger with a note on it. It said: 'Whoever opens this box will be killed!' Violet felt scared to open the box but she decided to open it. Inside the box was ... her mum!

Violet, for the first time ever, screamed so loud. She ran up to Charlie's room and told him to come downstairs.

'I don't believe it, our mum is dead!' Charlie said.

Violet cried so much she said unhappily, 'How could someone do this to our mum?' Suddenly there was a blackout. No one could see a thing. Everything was pitch-black, dark ...

Yasin Samad (10)
Cyril Jackson Primary School, Limehouse

Skeletons From The Dead!

One day a girl lived in a small house. She slept for a few hours at 10pm. When the time flew by at midnight she suddenly woke up and heard water dripping from the tap. She went to the kitchen to get some water. When she turned on the tap nothing came out.

A few seconds later she noticed a drop of red blood, she thought it was just the pipe but it was blood. She shouted. She was hallucinating so she went back to her room sand started to fall asleep. Suspiciously the TV switched on by itself.

When she went to switch off the TV the power went out and she panicked then sat in the corner of the room. She noticed the door was opening through the mirror. She was brave enough to see what was pushing the door so she slowly opened the door and a pile of skeletons fell out of the door. She was screaming loud enough for their neighbours to hear. She ran upstairs to her mum's room and closed the door.

After a few seconds of silence she whispered, 'Mum, are you there?' But no one replied. She pulled off her mum's quilt cover but all she saw was one of the skeletons that was hiding in there.

Something tapped her on her shoulder. When she turned around there was a headless man with a metal bladed axe ready to kill her …

Sultan Ahmed (10)
Cyril Jackson Primary School, Limehouse

The Pumpkin Man

One day on Halloween a boy and girl called Zack and Vanessa were carving a pumpkin. They had finished carving it but Zack accidentally made it come to life when he was trying to light it up with his powers. But it was evil. They tried to stop it but they couldn't.

So every Halloween it haunts that house and it will never leave that house ever!

Ashfaq Choudhury (10)
Cyril Jackson Primary School, Limehouse

Deathly Cold

Alfred needed a pee. He strode along the gloomy corridor, his footsteps echoing through the darkness. It was the end of a long day. A light flickered further down the corridor. As he reached the toilet door, everything went cold. Alfred shivered. He pushed the dirty metal door open.

The floor was wet; one of the sinks had been flooded. It was absolutely freezing. There was a threatening stain stretched up one wall.

He entered the cubicle. As he locked the door, he heard a whispering from outside; weird because he could have sworn it was empty.

Suddenly the whole frame of the cubicle shook violently, throwing Alfred off the seat. He muttered a single four-letter word.

It was so cold! Sweat dripped down his goose-pimpled face. He flushed and hurried out of the cubicle. It was like the pipes were whispering to themselves. The cracked mirrors were freezing up and Alfred could no longer see his pale reflection. A light flickered, sparks flew. The room was momentarily thrown into pitch-blackness.

Something cold closed round his neck, lifting him up into the air. Something was strangling him but it was invisible. He couldn't breathe and the freezing hands didn't loosen; he started to black out; his head felt like it was going to explode. The last thing Alfred heard was a harsh, icy laugh. The body fell to the floor, deathly cold.

Ed Budds (13)
Diss High School, Diss

The Shadows

The shadows of darkness, where the worst of everything hides and nothing is what it seems. For those who dare venture there, gone, is all I can say! No one knows what really happens. It just sits there toying with your mind and imagination, never revealing anything - until it's too late.

The girl in the street, she walked to her death. It's the way they hold themselves, nervous, alone, even glancing back as if expecting it. I ran after her only before I could reach her she turned the corner, into the dark alleyway beyond. I rushed round but when I got there all that was left to the once walking silhouette was a damp alleyway filled with rubbish, cardboard boxes and the smell of rotting fish, caught in my throat. She had gone, but where? That was just one of the many questions echoing in my head, while fear gripped me then coursed through my veins.

There was no time to dwell on the matter any further, however as a shadowy figure loomed over me from behind, grabbing me tight and pulling me in until I became one with the darkness that had moments earlier consumed the girl. Before she was the hopeless one that I tried to save then I was the helpless one but no one was around to help me - or at least try.

Kia Duly (14)
Diss High School, Diss

Scratch

Scratch. It wasn't the first time he had heard it. He heard it every night, *scratch,* slowly getting louder. His phone chimed a cheery tune, the exact opposite of what he was feeling. The phone offered some resistance to the ever present dark. He opened the message: 'I'm coming to get u, sender 666'. As soon as he had read it his phone cut out. He knew he should have recharged it. Oh well, too late now. Darkness fell like a shroud, thick and heavy. He was terrified.

Scratch, scratch. He hoped it was just a rat, just a big, furry, scary, gnaw off your fingers rat. Not a monster, certainly not a monster that could text.

Tap, tap, tap. He looked towards the window. Closed, with curtains drawn as usual but something was different. A shadow. A humanoid shadow. Suddenly it disappeared.

Bang! The sound came from the ceiling. *Bang!* This one was louder. *Crack.* A hole appeared in the ceiling. The boy was tense with fear, prepared to scream, petrified. Something dropped, a rat.

'Phew!' It was no bigger than the toy rat he kept in his cupboard. Why was he scared of a stupid rat?

Then it grew, morphing, changing, engulfing the boy. He had no time to scream.

Blackness. Death.

Thomas Dowden (14)
Diss High School, Diss

The Girls' Haunted Room

The girls and their dolls were tightly packed in the cupboard. In the pitch dark they could not see him but they knew he was there, they had seen his shadow haunting this room before. They didn't dare to breathe, didn't dare to whisper. Because if they did they knew he would hear it and their cover would have been blown.

The girls waited for someone, anything to come and comfort them. But instead the only comfort they felt was his cold air blowing through the keyhole. The girls knew the only way to get rid of him was to switch on the light, but they did nothing.

They did not know how he got to be there, all they knew was that he came every night and didn't leave until the sun rose and shone through the windowpane.

He got his pleasures from enveloping children, sucking out their spirits and gulping their flesh down his dead body. Maybe he was jealous of the life they had, maybe it was because they were happy. Whatever the reason he wanted to snatch the lives of these little girls.

It was morning, the sun shone through the keyhole. The girls thought it was safe to get out so they stepped out of the cupboard with no hesitation, little did they know he was just around the corner and as quickly as you could say, 'Death is here,' the girls were gone.

Mary Lambert (14)
Diss High School, Diss

Don't Look Back

'Don't look.'
'Never look.'
''Cause when you look it grabs you.'

It was so saddening, the silence alone in my living room. My parents were out and I was alone. Or at least I should be.

I made my way to the kitchen and poured myself a glass of water. The water made a slight trickling sound as it entered my cup. It took my mind off the silence for a little while but as soon as I sat down in the living room it hit me. I wasn't alone.

I edged my way around the room, keeping close to the wall. I gradually began to loosen up and sat down again. Although the TV was completely opposite the door, I couldn't take my eyes off the doorway which brought a slightly gloomy feeling.

Suddenly a black silhouette came out of the murky darkness. There were no features on the figure. At this point I was curling up under some cushions praying that it was just my parents.

The figure became less distinct and faded into the darkness. As I turned back to the TV to watch the news a very small rat-looking creature scurried behind the sofa from the doorway. I peered behind but saw nothing. I flashed a light down underneath the sofa and saw nothing but old chewing gum wrappers.

Quick as a flash it launched into the kitchen. Determined to kill it, I went in equipped with a cushion. I never left that kitchen.

David Phillips (13)
Diss High School, Diss

Corridors Of The Dead

Jonathon White was too hot. He wiped the sweat off his forehead and looked around for somewhere to hide from the hot Sicilian sun. He spotted a cool-looking entrance to a building and wandered towards it. As he got closer to the building he realised what it was. He had seen it on postcards in the hotel lobby. It was the Capuchin Catacombs; the place where the dead were kept.

Jonathon was intrigued. He walked into the building and was greeted by a friendly Italian who sat behind a table with a moneybox on it. Jonathon dropped a Euro on the table and walked through the door.

The sight that met him was terrifying. Hundreds of dead bodies hung from the walls like ghastly portraits in a haunted house. Skulls grinned at him like madmen and dried-out corpses had faces screaming twisted screams. Dull eyeballs stared blankly, their blinking days over.

The worst thing was the vast number of them. There was corridor after corridor; a huge maze for the dead. It would be far too easy to get lost in here and Jonathon was well aware of it.

The door clicked shut behind him. He slumped. Slowly he stepped forward, nervously. He didn't dare look left or right.

Jonathon reached the end of the corridor and turned right, then left, left, right, left ... he suddenly decided he'd had enough. He wanted out but as a cold bony hand clasped his shoulder he knew that wasn't possible!

Theo Perrin (13)
Diss High School, Diss

The Moving Darkness

When darkness creeps into the orphanage bedtime is nigh. The brother and sister, dumped into a child's worst nightmare, looked at each other; they knew what was lurking around these walls.

During the night, the kids awake were waiting, expecting, anticipating. Suddenly, noises from downstairs. There were just creaks, then they suddenly heard bangs!

They quickly got out of their room to see what was happening. Quickly, they looked down the corridor where they were. Swiftly, they turned and ran. They followed, the chase was on. They darted down the hallway. They were on their tail.

But then the sister fell, she had been caught! The brother looked back helplessly. The sister screamed, she then somehow broke free and ran as fast as she could to the stairs. But, trudging up the stairs they were coming, the kids were surrounded!

The brother went into the closet and his sister followed suit. They were trapped. The sister was scared, she turned round to her brother, he was also scared. There was banging against the big wooden door. They broke in and there they were, The Shadows!

They reached out, the brother and sister cried, that was the last thing they did. They were now part of the moving darkness, just a mere shadow. They joined many more children consumed over the years by The Shadows. Who was next?

Aaron O'Brien (14)
Diss High School, Diss

Dead End

It was a dead end. My screams, like needles, were piercing my skin. There was no way out and I knew it. She was behind me. Slowly I turned around daring myself to face her. She was still. Silent. Blue circles surrounding deep, dark eyes. Greasy, black hair. A thin body, draped sloppily in dirty rags. Chapped lips smiling cruelly at me. Long, yellow nails eagerly waiting to get me in their clutches.

She waited patiently, knowing that in a few moments she would be deeply satisfied.

The darkness seemed to replace my soul as I found myself staggering towards her. I stopped. I searched desperately for a way to escape the cruel terror that awaited me. Then I realised that this was my fate. I was to die brutally at the hands of a treacherous evil monster. The thin strand of my life was about to be cut.

I could feel the life being sucked from me. I grew weaker and weaker. She just stared greedily at me. I tried to resist the desire to give up, though it was just too painful. Her bare feet moved slowly towards me. I fell helplessly to the floor.

What was going to happen to me? Was I going to die? Disappear or just shrivel into nothing? I imagined my blood on her hands, my cold, dead body lying limply on the floor. I hoped her next victim would be stronger than me. I shut my eyes.

Jessica Cooper (14)
Diss High School, Diss

Night Creeper

When the sun sets no one is safe. There in the darkness the sinister shadow looms over you, like a skyscraper towering over a city.

How it got there nobody knows. All they know is what it does. At the dead of midnight it creeps through the streets, attracted by calm happy dreams. It slithers into your house silently.

It approaches the stairs … swiftly it moves, getting closer to your door. The door is slowly opened as the stealthy predator approaches its prey. Gazing down at you he intercepts your innocent dreams and twists them into frightful nightmares.

It can feel your heartbeat increasing. *Thump, thump!* The peaceful rise and fall of the victim's chest becomes more rapid. You scream, shout, thrash around in your bed when finally …

Your eyes snap open. You blink, as the door creaks shut. The sun has risen. The horrible night creeper has gone. All is safe until the darkness reappears.

Repelled by the light it returns to the shadows where it belongs. It watches … waits for its next helpless, unfortunate target.

Evan Hughes (13)
Diss High School, Diss

Young Writers Information

We hope you have enjoyed reading this
book - and that you will continue to enjoy it
in the coming years.

If you like reading and writing fiction drop
us a line, or give us a call, and we'll send
you a free information pack.

Alternatively if you would like to order further copies of
this book or any of our other titles, then please give us a
call or log onto our website at www.youngwriters.co.uk

Young Writers Information
Remus House
Coltsfoot Drive
Peterborough
PE2 9BF
(01733) 890066